Lysandros sensed Rio watching him as he held his sister's gaze. He could feel her scrutiny burning his skin, setting fire to the passion that had simmered dangerously close to the surface the last time he'd kissed her.

"Rio," he began, turning to her, opening his hand to reveal the box his mother had just secretly given him. He moved closer to Rio, her brows pulled together in confusion. "Will you do me the honor of becoming my fiancée?"

The words came far more easily than he'd thought and he opened the box as Rio's eyes widened in shock. She looked down at the ring and then back at him, questions clearly running riot in her mind.

"But..." Her voice was barely a whisper and the whole room echoed with a heaviness of expectant silence.

Slowly he took her left hand, which shook, confirming she really was afraid of what he was doing. Carefully he slid the ring onto her finger. It was a perfect fit. She looked at him, the same shock he felt flooding her eyes. "I want us to be engaged."

Rachael Thomas has always loved reading romance, and is thrilled to be a Harlequin author. She lives and works on a farm in Wales—a far cry from the glamour of a Harlequin Presents story—but that makes slipping into her characters' worlds all the more appealing. When she's not writing or working on the farm, she enjoys photography and visiting historical castles and grand houses. Visit her at rachaelthomas.co.uk.

Books by Rachael Thomas

Harlequin Presents

A Deal Before the Altar
Claimed by the Sheikh
Craving Her Enemy's Touch
The Sheikh's Last Mistress
New Year at the Boss's Bidding
Hired to Wear the Sheikh's Ring
A Ring to Claim His Legacy

One Night With Consequences

From One Night to Wife
A Child Claimed by Gold

Convenient Christmas Brides

Valdez's Bartered Bride
Martinez's Pregnant Wife

The Secret Billionaires

Di Marcello's Secret Son

Visit the Author Profile page at Harlequin.com for more titles.

Rachael Thomas

SEDUCING HIS CONVENIENT INNOCENT

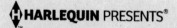

HARLEQUIN PRESENTS®

Recycling programs
for this product may
not exist in your area.

ISBN-13: 978-1-335-53818-5

Seducing His Convenient Innocent

First North American publication 2019

Copyright © 2019 by Rachael Thomas

Printed in U.S.A.

SEDUCING HIS
CONVENIENT INNOCENT

PROLOGUE

Spring in London

Lysandros Drakakis watched Rio Armstrong, the woman he wanted above all others, as she took her seat at the piano. An expectant hush fell over the room as everyone waited for the recital he'd arranged for his business clients at one of London's top hotels to begin.

Rio was beautiful. Her tall, slender body was full of poise and elegance and as she sat at the piano all eyes were on her. Everyone else in the room was waiting for her to play but all Lysandros could do was imagine her in his arms, kissing him with an unrestrained passion she'd so far resisted. Every time they'd kissed the hints of desire had lingered on her lips, tormenting him.

His younger sister, Xena, had introduced them, claiming them to be perfect for one another, and for the last two months he'd been the personification of a gentleman with this alluring beauty. He'd also been patient, allowing their relationship to unfold at Rio's pace. Not at all his usual style, but this was the first time since his disastrous engagement to Kyra ten years ago that he wanted to consider more than just physical gratification.

That uncharacteristic restraint since he and Rio had started dating was having serious side effects. Not having done anything more than kiss her, his mind was constantly filled with the image of their naked bodies entwined with desire, and as Rio's fingers began to caress the first notes of her performance from the piano, he closed his eyes, forcing himself to calm his ardour, try to halt the thoughts of her touching him, caressing him.

Rio had warned him, from the first moment he'd made his interest in her known, of her concert commitments, the need to put in hours of daily practice, and more recently had used those commitments as the reason she wasn't ready to take their romance further. But with summer approaching and the concert season ending, Lysandros was determined to whisk her away to his home in Greece. Once there he wanted to allow the attraction between them to bloom like the flowers on his island retreat.

A ripple of applause swayed around the room, dragging his thoughts back to the present. How long had he been wrapped in heated thoughts of making Rio his? Rio stood and took a bow, smiling at the audience's appreciation of her playing. She was a rising star in the world of classical music and small performances like this were her way of bringing the joy of the genre to new listeners.

As the audience slowly dwindled away, heading to the hotel restaurant or bar, he walked towards the large black grand piano where Rio was gathering up her music. She glanced up, smiling at him, and he could almost believe that she could be, as Xena had more than hinted at, the woman to overthrow all the disbelief in love with which his ex-fiancée Kyra had filled him.

'Excellent entertainment, Lysandros.' The gruff voice of Samuel Andrews, a man with whom he'd just signed a lucrative deal to supply his company with ten luxury yachts, invaded the moment.

'Indeed.' He glanced at the older man before looking over at Rio, who was almost ready to leave. He couldn't let her go without telling her how wonderfully she'd played—and arranging dinner tonight. 'If you will excuse me.'

He didn't wait for a response. The only thing that mattered now was being with Rio. In just a few days he would return to Greece, where he had a full schedule of meetings for the next few weeks, and it shocked him to realise how much he would miss Rio during that time. This was all such new territory for a man who'd done nothing but play the field for the last ten years.

Rio looked up at him, that sensual but shy smile on her lips convincing him further, if he needed it, that time together in Greece with this woman was exactly what he wanted.

'You were wonderful,' he said as he stood in the curve of the piano, its lid lifted. 'You play so beautifully.' He watched her, admiring her grace and elegance in the long black dress she wore, one shoulder bare, as the silky fabric swept across her breasts, a frill of black silk over her other shoulder. Her hair was pulled back at the nape of her neck in a tousled chignon he found so very sexy as he imagined setting it free during the passion of sex.

She gathered the last of her music up and clutched it to her, the softness of her brown eyes filled with happiness. 'Thank you.' Her voice was light and teasing, the sparkle in her eyes flirtatious. Finally, he was breaking through her reserve. Soon this innocent beauty would be his in the most intimate way. That thought intensified the heated lust already raging inside him after his imaginings while she'd played. 'Does that mean you will take me to dinner tonight?'

He stepped closer to her, not able to resist touching her, and brushed back a stray piece of hair, lifting her chin gently with his thumb and finger. His eyes held hers briefly, and then he brushed his lips over hers before answering. 'It most certainly does, especially as I have to return to Greece at the end of the week.'

'Next week?' Her voice was husky, proving she wanted him as much as he wanted her. 'So soon?'

'Yes, *agape mou*, so soon.' He wanted to take her in his arms and kiss her until that infernal barrier she hid behind came crashing down.

'I have to meet with Hans now, the conductor. He wants to go over some of the pieces with me, but afterwards I'll be free.' She paused. 'Free to make the most of the last few nights together.'

'Last few *nights*?' He couldn't miss the blush that had crept over her face or the sudden shyness that made her look at him from lowered lashes. He swallowed hard against the need to crush his mouth to hers, to kiss her until passion consumed them both, until desire doused them in flames.

'Yes, Lysandros.' Her whisper was husky and so very sexy. She moved closer to him, her gaze locked with his, the fire of their attraction almost crackling in the air around them. Did she have any idea what she was doing to him? How she was tormenting him? 'I want to be with you tonight. All night.'

He looked into her eyes, desire filling them, darkening the soft brown until they were almost black. 'Are you sure?' he asked softly, wanting her to know that he was willing to wait, that he understood this wasn't something she did lightly. He wanted her to know he was prepared to take things as slowly as she wanted to.

'Absolutely.' The certainty in her voice was all the reassurance he needed. Tonight, this beautiful woman, with an aura of innocence, would be his.

He kissed her gently, allowing her to taste his passion, his desire for her, and when she responded with as much need for him, he had to force himself to step back from her as the crazy need for her threatened to overcome him. 'I will make tonight very special for you, *agape mou.*'

'Just being with you will do that.' She blushed and hugged her music sheets tighter. 'But first I must sort this out.' She allowed the sheets of music to fall forward, as if providing the evidence for what she had to do. 'You know how hard Hans works us. And, besides, you need to mingle with your guests.'

He watched as she walked away, turning to look back at him, smiling, her step light with happiness. The same happiness that had made him feel a different man since he'd been dating Rio, sparking off conversations about engagement with his sister. Xena had been convinced that, ever since that first date with her friend, an engagement would be a question of when, not if.

Rio felt crazy and reckless with the anticipation of all that tonight would hold. Tonight she would give herself, give her virginity to a man who was everything she wanted. He might be her best friend's brother, might have already been engaged once, but he was the man who made her feel alive. Even though she knew he wasn't looking for any kind of long-term, emotional commitment, he was the man she wanted to be with above all others.

She pushed open the door of the grand room where practices were held and crossed the wooden floor to the piano, her heels echoing in the vastness of the room. Hans had insisted they go over some of her pieces for the final concerts of the season. She was early, so there was time to enjoy just playing, for no other reason than she wanted to.

She hadn't wasted time changing from her black gown. She'd wanted to get the meeting over and done with and back to Lysandros. For the first time in her life, she was irritated by the need to do such things, annoyed by the fact that it meant she couldn't be somewhere else, doing something else. Something else she was finally ready for. Even knowing Lysandros was only interested in her physically, she wanted to be with him, wanted to know the pleasure of a night in his bed.

As she sat at the piano she thought of Lysandros, of the way he'd kissed her before she'd left. Even if he hadn't promised her tonight would be special, it had been there in his kiss. Her heart fluttered with anticipation as she began playing, losing herself in the romance of the piece, letting all her emotion pour out through her fingers as she played.

As she ended the piece her whole body was humming with need for Lysandros. She closed her eyes and sat, hands lying on her lap as she savoured the moment.

'Now, *that* was beautiful.' Hans's voice came from behind her. Very close behind her.

She gasped and turned around, annoyed that he'd invaded her private moment. She felt vulnerable. Exposed. He'd watched her as she'd given free rein to her emotions, as she'd allowed all the desire she felt for Lysandros to pour into the music.

'You should have said you were there.' She couldn't keep the irritation from her voice.

'And ruin such a moment?' He looked at her, his gaze sweeping down her body. 'You looked so beautiful. So passionate.'

He stepped closer to her as he spoke and for the first time ever Rio felt threatened by a man's presence. The smell of alcohol hung around him and she didn't like the way he looked at her, the way he'd wiped away the purity of her feelings for Lysandros. Mentally she shook herself. She was overreacting. Embarrassed at being caught off guard.

'Shall we go through what you wanted to

discuss?' Desperately she tried to get the practice session back on track.

'Play something for *me*.' He seemed to be goading her. As if he'd known she'd been playing for someone else. For Lysandros.

She swallowed down her nerves, sure her embarrassment must be making her see things that weren't there. As she turned on the piano stool and sorted her music, she was aware of him moving even closer. She glanced over the grand piano towards the big bay window and the parkland beyond, which was coming to life now with spring. In the summer it would be full of people enjoying the sunshine. Now it was empty.

'That one,' he said as he leant over her shoulder, moving one piece of music to the front.

Play, she told herself. *Just play and he will step back.*

She took a breath and placed her fingers lightly on the keys. After a few seconds' pause, she began to play. At first it was stilted, emotionless as the uncertainty of the moment took over. He hadn't moved at all. Was she just being panicky? Gradually, even though he remained behind her, she began to relax, and the music flowed more naturally round the vastness of the domed room.

She finished the piece and sat looking at the keys, not daring to look up at him. When his hand rested on her bare shoulder she stiffened, her eyes wide. What was he doing?

She turned and looked at his hand, unable to move any other part of her body. She should get up, should step away, but she couldn't. Paralysed by fear, she dragged in a ragged breath.

As if her stillness had given consent, his hand moved lower, down over her chest, and she gasped, moving backwards on the stool, only to come against the firmness of his body.

'Don't,' she said, snatching at his hand as it slipped alarmingly lower. Inside the fabric of her gown. Instinctively she curled herself inwards, hoping the movement would prevent what he was trying to do, but the fabric slackened, enabling him to fully grasp her breast.

'What are you doing?' she shouted.

The room echoed with the sound as she tried to avoid him, but his grasp tightened painfully on her breast and she was trapped between his body and his arm. How could this be happening?

'I'm giving you what you want.' His voice had changed, become hard and menacing. His face was so close to hers now she could smell stale alcohol on his breath.

'No. No. This isn't what I want.' She struggled again and his grip on her tightened, his free hand now pressing down on her other shoulder.

'Don't be shy, Rio. I know you want it.' He groped at her breast. Pain shot through it. Sickness filled her. She had to stop this. Had to get away.

She pushed against the piano with a discordant jangle of keys. Her heels making it difficult, she scrambled to her feet. Finally, she was free of him, but so shocked by what had just happened she stood there, panting wildly as she looked at him.

Too late she realised her mistake. She should have run when she'd had the chance. He moved quickly, his body pressing hers against the keys, his mouth claiming hers in a cruel kiss. He roughly pulled her dress up, his hand grasping at her thigh as his body pushed her even harder against the piano.

The sound of her dress ripping galvanised her into action and she pushed against him. 'Get off.'

He was too strong for her. 'I like it rough,' he said as he tried to kiss her neck, his stubble scratching her skin, his foul breath making her retch.

'No,' she screamed as panic tore through her. He couldn't do this to her. He couldn't. She fought harder, screamed louder. 'No. Stop it.'

'What the hell?' Another voice mingled with her scream and Hans let her go. She sagged in relief as his weight suddenly moved away from her. Anger took over and she watched Hans being manhandled off her by two other members of the orchestra. Then shock set in. The whole thing had lasted only minutes, but it had felt like hours. Rio slithered to the floor, her arms clutching the piano stool as if she'd been cast into the sea and it was all she had to hold on to.

She rested her head on her arms, not wanting to watch now as the scuffle continued amidst Hans's angry accusations. How could he accuse her of leading him on? How could he say she had been up for it?

Tears slipped from her eyes. What had just happened?

'Are you hurt?' A woman's voice, gentle but filled with anger, made her lift her face. Rio glanced around the room like a scared rabbit. 'He's gone.'

'Thank goodness.' She shivered, the shock of her ordeal really taking effect now. 'God knows what he would have done if you hadn't shown up.'

'Evil bastard,' the woman snapped. 'Thank heavens the room was double-booked and that I had Philip and Josh with me.'

'Double-booked?' She looked up in confusion, not really knowing where she was any more. Nothing seemed to make sense.

The older woman placed her jacket round Rio's shoulders, which, instead of comforting her, only made her shiver even more. 'Don't worry about that now. Just be safe in the knowledge that as soon as the police get here he will be locked up and will never be able to do this to you or anyone else again.'

'What do you mean?' Her eyes were wide with fear and shock, tears threatening once again.

'The police will need your statement, as soon as you are able to, that is.'

'The police?'

'Yes. I called them whilst Philip and Josh wrestled him off you.' There was a hint of humour in the older woman's voice now and Rio gave a weak smile, finally realising who the woman was. Judith Jones, one of the company's newest members, a fabulous conductor and now her saviour.

Rio tried to stand, the ripped front of her dress falling away. She gasped in shock. Had he done that to her? Hans? 'My dress.'

Judith hugged her. 'The dress isn't important, Rio. All that matters is that we found you in time.'

Rio sniffed as the reality of Judith's words sank in. 'If you hadn't come along…' The implication hung in the air.

'But we did,' she soothed. 'And you can give your statement to the police.'

'Yes,' Rio said shakily.

'After you have done that, you will come to my home. I will personally take care of you tonight—unless there is someone else you'd rather be with, because you shouldn't be alone.'

'No,' Rio whispered sadly. How could she go to Lysandros now? After all she'd just promised him? She couldn't spend the night with him now. How could she even see Lysandros, let alone begin to tell him what had happened? Xena was busy this evening, and there was no way she could tell her yet either. 'No, no one is home tonight.'

'That's settled, then. You will stay with me,' Judith said firmly.

Rio smiled weakly. She should be with Lysandros tonight, should finally be discovering the joy of giving herself to a man. But how could she do that now? How could she allow any man to touch her again? Even the man she was beginning to fall in love with?

CHAPTER ONE

IT HAD BEEN six weeks since Rio had seen Lysandros. Six weeks since she'd said to him with her new-found flirty confidence that she wanted to spend all night with him. And six weeks since her world had been torn apart, destroying that confidence, ending her fragile hope that she and Lysandros could be beginning something special.

That life-changing moment after the recital had left her no option but to stand up the man she'd lost her heart to, the man she'd been ready to give everything to. She'd ended things between them, refusing to see or speak to Lysandros. That afternoon had been the last time she'd played the piano, the events that had unfolded as Hans had arrived in the practice room now making it impossible for her to go near a piano, let alone play.

Now another life-changing event meant that

at any moment Lysandros would come striding into the hospital room where his younger sister—her best friend, Xena—lay sleeping, looking battered and bruised from the car accident late last night.

'Xena.' Lysandros's voice snapped Rio from her thoughts as he surged through the door of the dimly lit private hospital room, his focus completely on the sleeping form of his sister.

Rio's heart pounded hard as she watched, almost in slow motion, Lysandros walk back into her life. She couldn't move, couldn't speak, couldn't make her presence in the large comfortable chair in the corner known. Instead she watched as he stood on the other side of Xena's bed, looking down at his sister. His stubble-covered jaw clenched, giving away the hurry in which he must have left Athens. He spread a hand over his chin as if he was trying to gain control, trying to work out what to say, what to do. He still hadn't even realised she was there.

With a sense of desolation more profound than she could have ever dreamed possible, Rio sat silently, watching the man to whom she'd lost her heart. As if that very thought made her presence felt, he turned to look at her, the emptiness in his eyes breaking her heart.

'Rio?' For a moment he seemed speechless, unable to say anything. 'When did you get here?'

'Early this morning.' She didn't know what to say to him. The way he searched her face, looking into her eyes for the answers she couldn't give him—answers about more than what had happened to Xena—almost tore her heart in two.

'How much longer is she likely to sleep?' His voice was firmer now, his shock at seeing her gone, as he walked to the bottom of his sister's bed. His height dominated the room, crowding her thoughts. The dark grey suit he wore only emphasised his muscular physique, reminding her how it had felt against her body when he'd kissed her. It had felt good. Right. But that had been before. That had been when she'd been a different person.

Aware that he was waiting for an answer, she dragged her thoughts back in line and resisted the urge to stand up and try to match his height. Instead she remained seated, hoping it would give off the message that she was as totally unaffected by him as she'd claimed when she had broken things off.

'When she first came round, she was very distressed. She couldn't remember anything, so the doctors gave her a sedative.' Rio focused her attention on Xena. She couldn't look at Lysandros. Not into those coal-black eyes. She didn't want to see the questions. The accusations. 'They said she will be sleepy for some time and are worried the knock on her head has affected her memory.'

'Her memory?' She had his full attention now. And the full force of his scrutiny.

'She doesn't recall the accident, or any other recent events, but as she knows who she is, the doctors are saying it's her way of coping. She is blocking it out.' Rio gulped back a wave of emotion. She had to be strong, had to focus on what Xena needed. Right now, nothing else mattered, not even her and Lysandros.

'What happened?' The question was firm, but by the look on his face she knew he was struggling to comprehend his sister's injuries, intensifying her own guilt at what she'd done to him. She didn't know how she was going to answer that and keep Xena's recent relationship from him. A relationship that was now over. It might be the reason why Xena was here in hospital, but it was no longer of any importance or relevance. Just as all she and Lysandros had shared was no longer of importance.

Last night, when Rio had arrived at Casualty, Xena hadn't recalled the promise she'd extracted from Rio. The promise not to tell Lysandros about her romance with Ricardo, a married man. A promise she'd never envisaged being brought into play, but last night Xena had been confused and distressed, unable to piece together recent events—or even Ricardo. The doctors had assured her it was almost certainly temporary, but it still upset Rio to see her friend like that and she knew she would do anything to make it better for her. Even keep the truth from her powerful and commanding brother. Just as she'd keep her true reason for ending their relationship from him.

Rio fought frustration and guilt as it welled up inside her. If only she'd been able to convince Xena that her married lover had ended the affair in order to make his marriage work. That he wouldn't leave his wife. Then maybe the accident would never have happened. Xena wouldn't be here now. But she hadn't been able to convince her. She and Xena had fallen out over it and Xena had slipped out after Rio had gone to bed and now Rio blamed herself for being too hard on her friend.

'What happened?' Lysandros demanded

again, his tone more insistent this time, dragging her back to the present.

'A car ran the lights. It hit her car hard. Spun it round.' As she thought of it, of the distress Xena must have felt, she closed her eyes, pressing her fingers to her temples. She was tired. Upset. Seeing Lysandros again was too much on top of Xena's accident.

'Are you okay?' Lysandros's voice was so close it made her jump.

She opened her eyes to see him crouched before her, his hands holding the arms of the chair either side of her. Trapping her. Instantly all she could think about was the moment Hans had trapped her against the piano. No, she couldn't allow that moment to rule her. Not ever. She just needed time to get over it.

'Rio?' Lysandros laid his palm on her lap, genuine concern in his voice. The heat of his hand grounded her, making her feel peculiarly safe.

She looked at him, almost bereft when he withdrew his hand, but this wasn't a time to focus on her or what she wanted or even needed. The only thing she had to do now was be there for Xena, doing and saying whatever she needed her to say.

'It's Xena who needs your concern, not me.' Even to her own ears, her voice sounded cold and emotionless.

He stood up, his long legs making him intimidatingly tall as he towered over her. She looked up at him, straight into the black depths of his eyes. She couldn't look away. Couldn't help herself wondering. Did the desire that had once filled them lie beneath their lacklustre darkness?

She forced her attention back to Xena's sleeping form, desperate to focus her emotions. She looked up at Lysandros again, the man she could have been so happy with if other things hadn't got in the way. 'I have spoken to the doctor. She should start to come round soon. Her broken arm and fractured wrist are expected to heal, although her injuries will mean she won't be able to play the violin for some considerable time.'

If only he knew the full truth of it all. Playing the violin would not be what Xena worried about as she recovered. It would be the loss of the man she loved that would fill her mind, her heart. If she remembered him. Tears sprang to Rio's eyes and she blinked rapidly to hold them back. Jumping up, she went to the window, looking out over the city bathed in glorious spring sunshine as the day began. Anything to get away from his scrutiny.

'Why?' He glanced at Xena, sleeping peacefully, blissfully unaware of the storm brewing around her. She'd promised Xena her secret would be exactly that until she was ready to tell anyone. With a clarity and determination she'd never felt before, Rio knew she would do whatever she had to for Xena. That was what friends did and she knew without a doubt that Xena would do the same for her.

She looked at Lysandros and refused to quake at the power that radiated from him, refused to bow to his superior command. This wasn't a business transaction—this was his sister's life. Xena's future. All Rio wanted was to be there for her.

'Even without the amnesia, the injuries Xena has sustained will require time to heal. She may not even be able to play when the new season starts in the autumn.'

Rio calmly laid the foundations, which, although true, was not the reason why Xena wouldn't want to rejoin the orchestra. Ricardo was part of the stage crew and amidst a torrent of tears Xena had clung to Rio before they'd fallen out, saying there was no way she could be part of the orchestra now. Rio's heart still broke to remember the pain in her friend's voice, knowing it came from losing the man she loved. A pain she also knew—because if she was truthful with herself, she had loved Lysandros.

'Then the best option is for Xena to return to Greece.' Lysandros looked at his sister, then back at her. The firm tone of his voice left her in no doubt that he did not expect his decision to be challenged—by anyone.

Rio had no intention of challenging him or his superiority. Relief flooded through her. If Xena left London and went to her island villa to recover, then any chances of gossip about her and Ricardo would be lessened. Ricardo certainly wouldn't be the one to say anything. He was a married man and stood to lose everything. Xena would be able to recover in peace, and although the thought of saying goodbye to her friend at such a time hurt, it was the best solution.

'Yes, I think that would be exactly what she needs in the circumstances.' Rio's voice had lost that determined edge, but she was acutely aware of Lysandros's scrutiny.

He moved back to the window, looking out over London for a moment before turning to face her. Like an animal trapped in the beams of car headlights at night, she froze to the spot. Was he going to demand an explanation? From her? Was he now about to demand to know why she'd stood him up that night?

'And what about you?' He spoke gently and she swallowed down her guilt. She didn't deserve his concern. She might not have been directly involved in the accident, but she blamed herself. 'I can see this is affecting you too.'

He moved closer to her, his handsome face softened by the kind of concern she guessed those he did business with rarely saw. She wanted to back away, wanted to keep as much distance between herself and this man as possible. But she couldn't. He mesmerised her, made her want things she couldn't have now.

'I will stay in London.' Her voice was barely more than a whisper. He reached out and pushed the stray strands of her hair back from her face, just as he'd done the last time he'd seen her. Before he'd kissed her.

She caught her breath. Her pulse raced so fast she couldn't say anything. All she could do was look into his hypnotically sexy black eyes.

'You have had a shock too. You shouldn't be alone.' His words were heavy with his Greek accent, making her body's reaction to him, to his nearness, even more intense.

She stepped back from him, away from the strange power he had over her. 'I will be fine here.'

'I am sure Xena wouldn't want that,' he insisted, his eyes dark and watchful, as if he was trying to tell her *he* wanted her there.

'No, I should stay here.'

Lysandros took in Rio's face, unusually bare of make-up, and along with the casual jeans she wore with a sweater, she had an air of complete innocence. What was it about this woman? Why did she affect him like this? Why did he want to take on the challenge she'd unwittingly issued when she'd stood him up and then told him it was over? Her response to his kiss after the piano recital had promised him so much. So what had changed that?

Xena stirred and he forced his mind from those questions. Instantly Rio was at his sister's side, her attention focused completely on her friend. He should be giving Xena the same attention, but he couldn't keep his eyes off Rio. Her hair, loosely pulled back, looked tousled, giving away the haste in which she'd obviously left her bed early this morning. She might well have been here for hours, but she looked beautiful. Breathtakingly beautiful. His heart wrenched.

'Lysandros is here,' Rio said softly as Xena opened her eyes, a look of bewilderment on her pale face.

Xena winced as she tried to slide up the partially elevated bed. Rio fussed with her pillows, going to great lengths to make them right. Anything, it seemed, to avoid looking at him. Anything to avoid that sizzle of attraction that still sparked between them, despite the current situation.

'Lysandros?' Xena asked shakily as she turned to look up at him.

'I came as soon as I heard,' he said, taking her hand in his. He knew Rio was watching him. Every nerve in his body was tuned in to her.

'But you only just returned to Greece,' Xena said weakly as she looked at him, then at Rio. Lysandros's heart sank. He'd been in Athens for the past six weeks. Xena obviously didn't remember much at all.

'Do you think I would stay there when I had just been told by Mother that you had been involved in an accident?' He glanced up at Rio.

'I was in an accident?' The panic-laced

question confirmed all Rio had just told him about Xena's memory loss.

'Yes,' Rio added gently, and Xena looked at her. 'A car accident.'

'I don't remember.' Xena shook her head. Then her eyes widened. 'I don't remember anything.'

'Don't panic,' Rio soothed, and Lysandros marvelled at her command in the face of Xena's fear. 'You've had a bump on the head. I'm sure it's perfectly normal not to remember things straight away. I'll go and find the doctor now, get him to come and reassure you.'

'Don't go yet,' Xena pleaded, and Rio hesitated. 'There is something else wrong, isn't there? Something is wrong between you two. I can feel it.'

'Don't worry about us,' Rio said soothingly, again fussing with the bedsheets.

Xena laughed softly. It was such an unexpected sound that Lysandros looked at his sister, not sure what was coming next. Tears maybe, as the shock of the accident set in.

'Well, I hope you two haven't fallen out.' Xena rested her head back against the pillow, her face as pale as the white sheets. 'Because you do realise you were meant for each other?'

Lysandros didn't dare look at Rio. It wasn't

just the accident Xena didn't remember; she didn't remember he and Rio were no longer dating. 'Of course we haven't fallen out. Far from it.'

He looked at Rio across the bed, shocked to find how near they now were. Their concern for Xena had drawn them physically so close he only needed to lean forward a little to kiss Rio. And he wanted to. She still had that effect on him, still raised the desire in his blood until it almost boiled.

'Fallen out?' Rio frowned, her gaze locked with his, and he saw the moment she realised what he was doing, that he didn't want to panic Xena or worry her by explaining they had done exactly that six weeks ago. He let out a breath of relief when she laughed softly, looking at Xena, apparently happy to conspire with him. 'Of course we haven't.'

Lysandros straightened away from the temptation of kissing Rio once more and looked at her. 'You will, of course, come to Greece with Xena. I'm sure it's what she will need to aid her recovery.'

Rio's eyes snapped to his. 'I don't think that is necessary,' she said firmly, a clear challenge in her voice.

Lysandros should be worried about Xena,

should be anxious about her amnesia, but all he could think about was getting Rio to his Greek island. Getting her alone. Then he could convince her that what they'd had before she'd stood him up had been good, worth continuing. He wanted Rio. Couldn't get her out of his mind. It was not just because she was the only woman to have stood him up. It was more than that. He couldn't make sense of his reaction to her. All he knew was that this might be the only opportunity to discover the pleasure of making her his.

Rio took a step away from the bed, away from him. As if she sensed his ulterior motives. As if she knew the reason he wanted her in Greece was because he couldn't accept that she didn't want him.

He damn well couldn't.

Not when desire had sparked within every smile she'd bestowed on him. Not when she had seductively let him know she was ready to take their relationship to a different level.

Even now, in the hospital, with his sister's suspected amnesia looking ever more likely, the air was filled with sexual tension, pulling him and Rio together, invalidating her claim they were over. How could he turn his back on something so powerful, something that had promised to be amazing? The disaster of his engagement had loomed over him for ten years, but whatever it was between him and Rio, this was the first time that shadow had been eclipsed.

'Xena, do you want Rio with you in Greece?'

'Most definitely,' Xena said, her voice still wobbly as she looked from one to the other, as if she couldn't make out what was happening.

'Then I will make arrangements immediately for you both to travel to Greece.' He turned to leave. He couldn't stand this close to Rio and not touch her, not try to convince her with a kiss that they needed to explore the attraction between them. They needed to extinguish the fire of desire and he knew exactly how. 'I will speak to a doctor right now.'

He strode out of the room, not expecting Rio to follow him, but he knew she had. He sensed it with every taut muscle in his body. He continued to walk briskly down the hospital corridor, wanting to be completely out of Xena's hearing before he turned to face the onslaught of Rio's anger. Anger that radiated up the corridor after him.

'Lysandros, will you wait?' She was angry all right. He turned slowly to face her, keeping his expression devoid of emotion. 'Why are you allowing Xena to think we are still together?'

'Because I don't wish to upset her.'

'I can't just go to Greece and pretend everything is right between us.' The defiant tilt of her chin should have annoyed him, but instead it set light to the fuse of lust once more. Why did this woman drive him so wild with desire? Her lack of experience with men had been evident from the first day Xena had introduced them. So why did he want her so much when he'd always preferred experienced women? The kind of woman who wouldn't demand anything more than a night of exquisite pleasure? No questions, no longing for happy endings, just hot, passionate nights until the desire cooled.

'Rio.' He'd always liked the feel of her name on his lips and moved closer to her. 'Xena needs you. You are her closest friend.'

She folded her arms across her slender body, adding to the aura of defiance—and the spark of lust in him.

'I should be playing the piano each day, even though the season is over.' He didn't believe the hostile glint in her eyes for one minute. Just as he didn't believe that excuse. There was an emptiness in it that warned him she was hiding something.

He smiled at her weak excuse. Was she afraid of what was between them? Afraid of its power? 'Xena has a grand piano in her villa, which I am sure she would love you to play.'

He didn't go on to say that he also had a piano in his Athens apartment. That would deter her further, but the thought of her playing it—just for him—fired his lust higher.

She shook her head. 'No. I need to stay in London.'

He moved closer still, putting temptation in his path once more. He couldn't allow that to distract him, not when he knew Xena would want her friend with her if she had to return to Greece. If she had to face the reality of not only her loss of memory but being unable to play her violin while her wrist and arm healed, she would need Rio.

He would need Rio there too. As hard as it was to admit, he found it difficult to emotionally connect with anyone, even Xena. Angered that his flaw had surfaced, that maybe it had chased Rio away, he drew on the few facts he knew about the accident.

'Why was Xena out alone when she wasn't familiar with driving in a big city at night?'

Rio's eyes sparked with anger, her soft lips pressing into a firm line. For a moment he thought she wasn't going to answer. 'I had no idea she'd gone. We'd…had words.'

'Was she meeting someone?' He might still want Rio in a way that unnerved him, but right now she was the only person who could help him understand what had happened last night.

'I think so.' He heard the pain in her voice and a twinge of guilt spiralled through him until he reminded himself he was doing this for Xena. She would have been furious with him for upsetting her friend, but he needed to know and right now Xena was unable to talk for herself.

He gentled his tone. 'Who?'

'Just a friend.'

'And what were you doing at this time?' He hated himself for needing to know just where Rio had been that night. Xena had assured him Rio hadn't dated anyone else since their split and he'd accepted that, had given Rio the space she'd asked for. Maybe now he'd get the answers he wanted, maybe even continue where they'd left off.

'I went to bed, assuming Xena had too.' Rio looked boldly at him, daring him to challenge her explanation. And he would. He hadn't got where he was now in business by not taking risks. His world-renowned luxury yacht company had pushed him to the limits and beyond as he'd fought to bring his father's declining shipping company into the twenty-first century and expand it. There was no way he was going to allow Rio to undermine him. He wouldn't allow her to keep him from the truth about last night—or any other night, for that matter.

'You said you'd had words. What about?' His usually all-too-effective charm slipped into his voice and he watched as a flurry of emotions crossed her face.

'It doesn't matter now.'

He hadn't expected that. 'And why would that be?'

She inhaled deeply then moved a pace towards him. A valiant attempt at bravado.

'It was nothing; you don't need to concern yourself.' He hadn't anticipated the innocent and somewhat shy Rio Armstrong to have such a sting in her tail.

'My sister is lying in a hospital bed, unable to recall the accident and obviously other things too. I have every right to concern myself.' He looked back up the corridor to where

Xena's private room was, giving weight to his argument.

'We were talking about a man.' She paused as if contemplating her next words carefully. 'That's all you need to know.'

So Rio *had* spurned him, only to move on to a new lover. 'And this man is the reason you stood me up?' He waited for her answer, the unexpected turn in the conversation working in his favour.

'That's not important now.' Rio skilfully avoided the issue, but he wasn't going to let her get away with not answering him that easily.

'Why did you stand me up, Rio?' The need to know surged forward, pushing all other thoughts to one side. 'Because you kissed me? Told me you wanted to spend the entire night with me?' He taunted her mercilessly.

She gasped, her gaze meeting his, indignation in her eyes. 'No.'

'Why did you change your mind?' If only she could admit there was something between them. 'What are you afraid of, Rio?'

'I'm not afraid of anything. I simply don't want a man in my life—any man.' Sparks of anger filled her words, but he refused to allow them to penetrate his armour. He'd do precisely what he'd done for the last six weeks and wait for the right moment. This was a conversation to have later, in Greece, on the island, when she would have no option but to talk to him.

'Xena would want you to come to Greece and help her through this difficult time.' He pushed home his point, satisfied when he saw her conflicted expression. 'The last thing Xena needs right now is to think you and I have fallen out. Whatever has happened between us, we owe it to her to be there for her in Greece—as a couple.'

Rio wanted to crumple to the floor. She was ensnared in a trap of her own making. Damn Lysandros. He'd led her right to it and she'd obliged, stepping in. Yet despite all this she knew he was right. Xena would need her, and if that meant going to Greece and pretending she and Lysandros were still together, then that was exactly what she would do. Not because Lysandros had asked her but because of the bond of friendship between her and Xena.

Lysandros had a business to run and she knew he preferred to spend his time in Athens, where he notoriously played as hard as he worked. Surely he would return to that life once Xena was settled into her island villa?

Surely he wouldn't pursue her or the promise she'd once made. Not when he could have any woman he wanted.

'That's unfair,' she defended herself as he regarded her from dark and unyielding eyes. If only he wasn't so striking, so handsome. If only he didn't make her heart flutter so wildly. If only she didn't find him so attractive and hadn't almost given herself so completely to him. 'I'd do anything for Xena.'

His brows rose in disbelief. 'Except come to Greece and spend the summer with her—because of me.'

'You really are very arrogant.' She grappled with the way he made her body tingle as he moved closer. He searched her face, his eyes darkening, reminding her of the moment she'd told him she'd wanted to spend the entire night with him.

Her pulse leapt wildly as that moment clashed with this, confusing her after his annoyance. She wanted to turn away, wanted to conceal the attraction she had for him, but she couldn't. As hard as she tried, she couldn't fight the way he made her feel.

'Right now, all that matters is that Xena gets well and regains her memory.' Rio forced herself to look away from the handsome Greek who was wrong for her on so many levels. She couldn't allow herself to fall for him all over again. She didn't want that kind of power held over her.

'As soon as the doctor tells me she is well enough to travel, we will go.' His deep and sexy accent sent ripples of awareness over Rio, but she refused to feel them, refused to react.

'What if I agree—just for a while?' She was torn between what Xena needed and protecting her fragile heart.

'Not for a while, Rio. For the entire summer,' Lysandros added with icy calmness. 'That is what Xena will want—and need.' He knew she wouldn't refuse to give Xena what she needed. Damn him.

'No, I can't.'

'But you will come, won't you, Rio? Because you will do anything to help your friend.' Rio couldn't believe how he was manipulating the situation—or the way her body reacted just from having him near her. Had she been too hasty in ending it all after what Hans had done? Would Lysandros have understood if she'd told him?

The questions chased each other through her mind. There was no way she could have told him, not when their relationship had been nothing more than just another affair to him. She'd never been foolish enough to believe otherwise.

'Very well. I will, but not because you have asked, or should I say bullied, me to do so, but because I want to be there for Xena.'

The look he gave her made Rio realise that everything she'd ever been afraid of happening if she saw him again was happening. She was still attracted to him. Still wanted to be with him, but things had changed. Things he didn't know about—couldn't know about.

'And because we have things to sort out?' The question sounded casual, but the look in his eyes was far from that.

'We don't have anything to sort out. We won't even need to see one another.' Rio folded her arms, desperate to stand her ground, prevent her body from betraying her.

'Xena believes we are together. I don't think making her worry about us will help her recovery, Rio, and we will be seeing each other, of that you can be sure.'

CHAPTER TWO

FOR TWO DAYS, Xena's Greek island retreat had been a haven of tranquillity for both Rio and Xena. Now Lysandros was due to arrive from Athens and Rio's nerves were threatening to get the better of her. He'd be disappointed his sister's memory of the accident and previous weeks hadn't yet returned.

Rio glanced at Xena, compassion for her friend's predicament filling her. Xena didn't recall anything that had happened in the weeks leading up to the accident. She had blocked out everything bad. Ricardo's rejection of her. The assault Hans had attempted on Rio. The break-up between Rio and Lysandros. Even blocked the accident itself. Xena lived under the illusion that none of those things had happened.

'It's so frustrating,' Xena said as she looked up at Rio. 'Why can't I remember anything?'

Rio sat down beside Xena. 'It will come. The doctor said you just need time—and rest.'

'I can remember that Lysandros will be back from Athens today and we are all going to visit my mother,' Xena said brightly, recalling the arrangement that had been made as they'd arrived on the island.

Rio, too, could remember that Lysandros was due to return to the island today, but for very different reasons.

'Maybe you could play a little,' Xena said, pulling Rio from her thoughts. 'It might help me remember something.'

Rio looked at the grand piano, forlorn and abandoned since they'd arrived. 'Later, perhaps,' she soothed, trying hard not to let her fear of even going near it show.

'I am rather tired.' Xena stifled a yawn. 'I think I will go and have a lie-down before we visit my mother. Gather my strength again.'

Rio watched her friend go with a heavy heart. If only there was something more she could do to help. She missed the confident and bubbly girl Xena really was.

For the past two days, while Lysandros had been in Athens, it had been easy to allow Xena to think that she and her brother were still a couple. But once he was here, it wouldn't be so easy. She was still far too attracted to him, still longed for the dream of happiness she'd glimpsed before it had been cruelly snatched away by Hans.

With a sigh of frustration she turned and walked to the large glass doors that opened up onto the terrace with a view of the sea. As she looked out over the sparkling waters she saw the sleek white speedboat slowing and moving towards the island. She pushed her thoughts aside, watching as Lysandros stepped onto the jetty. Her heart leapt as he looked towards the villa and she quickly moved out of view. She didn't know if she could do this, even though deep down she wanted nothing more than to go back to that moment after the recital.

Footsteps sounded on the marble floor as Lysandros entered his sister's villa. Rio forced brightness into her voice that didn't echo in her body despite the idyllic Greek island setting and the early summer sunshine.

'Hello, Lysandros.' She kept her voice firm, refusing to allow her nerves to show in any way. Whatever Xena believed about them, she needed to keep him at a distance and he had to know that.

'Hello, Rio.' The cool edge to his voice contrasted sharply with the darkening of his eyes as his gaze swept over her, creating a trail of tingles almost impossible to ignore.

Power radiated from him and despite his relaxed attire she knew he was anything but. The hard line of his clean-shaven jaw gave so much away. The courage she'd managed to summon up during the first days on the island began to slip away like the retreating tide. How could she be around him and be indifferent to him?

'How is Xena?' He moved a little closer, convincing Rio he knew she was still attracted to him.

'She has gone for a lie-down.' Rio let out a slow breath of relief as he walked away from her, giving her some much-needed physical distance between them.

'Has she remembered anything yet?'

Rio shook her head. 'Nothing.'

'Nothing?' She heard the despair in his voice. Despair that matched her own.

'She sounded so frustrated when we talked on the phone,' he said as he walked towards the baby grand piano. Did he have to bring it so starkly to her attention?

'It is frustrating for her.' Rio watched Lysandros, the man who still held her heart if only she was brave enough to give it to him, as he turned and frowned at her.

'I understand that.' He spoke again, snagging her attention back to him. 'But it's just as frustrating for me to know how much this is worrying her.'

'This is a big ordeal for Xena,' Rio said, watching Lysandros as he stood by the piano looking out towards the sparkling sea beyond the garden of the villa. He resembled a predatory wild cat, intent on luring its prey ever closer. Or was she imagining him drawing her in? 'She's lost some of her memory, maybe even her career, and she can't even pick up her violin and seek solace in playing.'

'Xena tells me you don't play either, even though you claimed daily practice was essential.' The sound of waves rushing onto the soft sand beyond the villa punctured the silence as she met the suspicion in his eyes. He was throwing her reason for not wanting to leave London back at her.

As he looked at her the hot sultry air suddenly crackled with undeniable tension between them. That strong attraction she had to ignore but was finding it ever more difficult to. He knew it too. He was far too astute, far too in control to be easily fooled.

'It's true. I should be practising every day.' She paused as she thought of Hans, of what he'd believed she'd wanted. Hans had been so adamant she had been leading him on, giving him the come-on. She hadn't been able to touch the keys, let alone play, since then. The piano and that moment were far too painfully linked. Even though she knew she'd done nothing to encourage him, she couldn't bring herself to sit at the piano, let alone play it.

Neither was she ready to tell Lysandros why she'd stood him up, why she'd coldly ended their relationship when it had been so good, so right. Xena didn't recall how she'd consoled Rio, how she'd tried to persuade her to tell Lysandros, and right now that suited Rio. She needed to avoid that painful conversation for as long as possible.

'So why are you not practising, Rio? Xena loves to hear you play. As do I.' He began to walk towards her, stopping when she backed away.

'I… I…' she faltered, not knowing what to say without telling him exactly why she didn't want to go near the piano.

'At least you can still physically play the piano—if you choose to.'

His accusation hit home and she dragged in a breath. Did he have to make her feel worse?

Play on the guilt she felt about the night of the accident? About him? Them?

'This isn't about me. This is about Xena.' Desperately she pushed back her pain, her raw emotions, trying to bring the conversation back to Xena.

He took another step towards her, bringing him so close she could smell the citrus tang of his aftershave, and it made the memory of their last kiss collide with the guilt for all Xena was going through, as well as her own fear. She tried not to recall how light-headed Lysandros had made her feel when he'd smiled at her, reminding herself he was well versed in the art of charming women.

Yet he'd been prepared to take things slowly with her. At first, she'd thought it was simply because of her friendship with Xena, but soon she'd wondered if it was more than that. He'd respected her. He'd showed patience and kindness totally in contrast to the playboy past Xena had told her about. He'd treated her as if she was special.

'Is it, Rio?' His voice had deepened, become so sensually soft he could be seducing her.

'Of course it is. I'm here for Xena, not myself—or us. Not that there is an us any more.'

'What happened after the recital, Rio? What

are you keeping from me?' His question hung in the air and she hated the way he made her feel, the way she wanted to confide in him, tell him what had happened. But she couldn't. It was over between them and there was no point in going over that night now. She was here only for Xena.

'There is nothing to tell,' she said quickly, hoping he wouldn't keep asking, be able to tell she had been doing exactly that.

'Let's take a walk on the beach while Xena is resting.' He changed the subject so fast Rio felt dazed.

'Xena and I are due to visit your mother today.' She grasped at that. 'Maybe we should wake Xena now.'

'As I am the one charged with the task of getting you both there, we can spend a while walking on the beach first.' He paused and looked at her, the intensity in his eyes changing, making her pulse leap with awareness she wasn't sure she was ready to acknowledge yet.

'I ought to leave Xena a note. In case she wakes.' Rio began to write a quick note and Lysandros stood over her, so close her body began to tremble, not with fear, as she'd expected, but with anticipation. Need. For him.

'Make sure you mention you and I are together.' His voice had dropped to almost a whisper and was so sexy she had to close her eyes against the tingle that rushed up her spine.

She put the pen down and turned, her gaze locking with his, holding it.

Lysandros knew Rio was keeping something from him. He'd known it since he'd first arrived at the hospital after the accident. He'd seen it in her eyes. Sensed nervousness in every move she'd made. Now that Rio was here with Xena, he was going to get to the bottom of what had happened the night she'd left him waiting alone at a romantic and secluded table for two.

The sunshine was gaining in strength as he stepped out of the villa, across the terrace and onto the sand. Beside him Rio adjusted her hat, and while he accepted it was necessary to protect her pale complexion from the sun, he sensed it was much more about erecting a physical barrier between them. He put on his shades. If the way his body was reacting to her nearness was anything to go by, the more barriers between them the better. For now at least.

'What really happened the night of the accident?' He plunged right in as swiftly as if he'd just dived into the cool waters from his yacht.

'I told you. A car ran a red light and hit Xena's.' The defensive tone of those short, sharp sentences gave so much away, but that wasn't what he wanted to know.

'I know the details of the accident itself.' He couldn't keep the impatience from his voice. He had to know just why his sister had been driving around London alone so late at night.

'So why ask?' He sensed her looking at him, but he kept his focus ahead, sure that if he didn't put her under the spotlight she would tell him the finer details of that treacherous night.

'Because I'm Xena's brother and I want to know what happened before the accident.'

Her pace faltered and she stopped, forcing him to do the same, but she didn't look at him. Instead she stared out to sea. Yet another avoidance tactic. 'There is nothing more to tell.'

'Are you sure, Rio?' The question caught her attention and she turned to face him. He wished she didn't have her sunglasses on, wished he could see the expression and emotion in her soft caramel-brown eyes.

She sighed and he watched the smooth, pale skin of her throat move as she swallowed. At least he could now be certain he was finally near the truth. 'You might be able to manipulate others into doing what you command, but it won't work with me.'

The passion in her voice was intense and she moved away, holding her hat in place against the playful, warm wind. Her long limbs were outlined as the wind flattened the blue sundress against her, testing his resolve far too much. He couldn't allow himself to be distracted by the attraction she still had for him. Not yet. Xena had to come first.

'Manipulate?'

'Yes, you try and control everything. Everyone. Even Xena.'

'I resent that accusation. What I do for Xena I do out of love.'

'Love?' She abandoned her attempts to hold her hat in place and took it off, exposing her subtly highlighted hair, which had been pulled back into a rough ponytail. The wind whipped stray strands of hair across her face and he scrunched his hands against the urge to push them back from her lovely and beguilingly innocent face.

Whatever it was that had changed things for Rio after the recital, he sensed she was fighting hard against her attraction to him. An attraction he still felt, still wanted to explore. Patience was all he needed.

'I don't think a man such as the mighty Lysandros Drakakis, CEO of Drakakis Shipping and Luxury Yachts, does anything for love, does he?'

Her taunt had the desired effect but he resisted the urge to respond with anger. He was well aware of his inability to emotionally connect with his sister or mother, let alone with another woman. Rio might have challenged that on so many levels, but he wasn't going to allow her to know it right now. 'Love for my family is an entirely different thing from passionate love. That kind of love is built on sexual attraction and heated desire.'

She blushed and looked away. He smiled at the sense of satisfaction that ruffling her feathers had brought him. That sexual chemistry was still there. Buried but alive. 'For you maybe.'

'So you are holding out for true love, are you? Is that why you stood me up so spectacularly? So publicly?'

He could still taste her rejection, something he wasn't at all used to. If he wanted a woman it was usually only a question of when, not if. Rio had refused point-blank to see him after that night, cementing her status as the first woman to turn him down. The only woman to wound his male pride since his early twenties, when his first taste of love had been soured by deceit.

'Yes, I am holding out for true love and you would hardly be the perfect candidate. Not with a string of broken hearts behind you.' She smiled in that *so there* kind of way the English were so good at. 'But I'm not here for us. In case you have forgotten, I'm here for Xena.'

'And what we had isn't of consequence?'

Rio looked uncomfortable and a heavy sense of seriousness filled the warm air around them. 'My friendship with Xena is more important than anything else. I don't want *us* to get in the way of that.'

She looked as though she was holding her breath, as though she was waiting for him to piece together whatever it was in her mind, but the mention of his sister served only to direct his thoughts back to his original purpose of bringing her out here to talk alone.

'I don't think going over the accident will help anyone right now. She has blocked out everything from the last two months. It's as if she is stuck at a happy point in her life.'

'I agree on that. That is why I believe it will reassure Xena if she thinks that we are in love.'

'In love? You and me?' She stumbled over

the words, her fingers fidgeting with the hat she clasped as if it were a lifeline. 'Is that really necessary?'

His mind raced. All his sister had ever wanted was for him to meet someone and fall in love, and the attraction between him and Rio had been so obvious, so intense he'd allowed Xena to revel in her role as matchmaker. Allowed her to believe there was a future for him and Rio. She'd even suggested that this time he should use their grandmother's engagement ring, saying that Rio wouldn't want the flashy diamonds Kyra had demanded.

He should have told Xena there and then that he didn't want any kind of commitment, but he hadn't wanted to destroy her happiness then, just as he didn't want to now. 'It would be what Xena has always wanted for us and maybe it could actually help Xena to feel more emotionally secure, which might enable her to remember things again.'

Rio's heart raced. How could she pretend to be in love with Lysandros when just being around him sent her pulse racing?

She sighed heavily, determined not to dwell on her problems but to focus on Xena and the heartache she had endured when Ricardo had ended their romance, and the worry of how she'd react when she remembered all about it. 'I'd do anything to help Xena, but pretending we are lovers?'

'What are you scared of, Rio?'

'I'm not scared of anything.' She swung round to face him square on, every muscle in her body tense as if ready for a fight, forcing her to remember a time and a man when a physical fight had been necessary. The clamour of her memories, the guilt of the accident and the secret she had to keep for Xena became one big storm cloud, fully laden and ready to spill everything out around her.

'Really?' His voice softened, and he moved closer to her. She thought he was going to touch her face, brush her hair back and then kiss her. Heaven help her, she wanted him to as much as she didn't.

She couldn't become enslaved by the attraction. She needed to divert his attention. 'You blame *me* for all that's happened to Xena, don't you?'

'I think you are doing an admirable job of that already.' His eyes were granite hard as his gaze fixed her to the spot.

She thought back to Xena's distress before the accident as she stepped back from Lysandros, needing the sparks of attraction to stop so she could think clearly. She could still hear the desperation in her friend's voice.

'Ricardo wants us to finish. He wants to sort everything out between him and his wife.'

'Rio.' Lysandros took her arms, turning her gently to face him, the heat of his touch sending skitters of awareness, mixed with trepidation, hurtling through her. She couldn't bear that she still had that kind of reaction to him. It was in total contrast to what she'd vowed after the attack. She just couldn't be at a man's mercy again and most certainly not one as powerful and attractive as Lysandros Drakakis. 'What are you keeping from me?'

Rio looked down and away from his scrutiny but he didn't let her go. When she looked up he was far closer than she had thought. Too close. She backed away as much as she could while his hands still held her upper arms, determined to show control and restraint.

'I'm not going to tell you anything if you don't let me go.'

He did as she requested, but his expression warned her not to push him further, not to test his patience. 'I apologise.' The words were sharp and accented, proving this whole situation with Xena was as upsetting for him as for her. Xena had often told her he was the ultimate big brother, kind and caring of his sister's needs, yet wildly overprotective, and he was now showing that.

'So you should.' She rubbed her arms, trying to brush away his touch, the memory it evoked and the reality of the very reason she'd stood him up. If she told him right now what had happened, would he understand? He was the kind of man who wanted instant gratification. Although he'd shown kindness and patience with her, courting her in a way she was sure he'd not done in many years, he was the worst kind of man for her to be attracted to now that her confidence was so low.

'Perhaps we should go back to the villa and see if Xena is ready to visit your mother.'

He swore harshly in his native Greek and she had no idea why. Quite apart from that, it was hard to focus on the conversation when each deep breath he took made his muscled chest expand, snagging her attention in a way she didn't want, warning her he was at his limit as well as reminding her what could have been if only she'd been brave enough.

'I need your help, Rio. I can't stand by and do nothing while Xena becomes more and more frustrated at not remembering.'

The unexpected openness of his words touched her heart. He might be many things, but he *did* care about his sister.

'I will help, Lysandros. That's why I'm here now.' She could feel her resolve melting the highest peaks of her defences, making them begin to slide away.

He moved closer to her and she held her breath as he took her hand in his, fixing those intensely dark eyes on her face. 'Xena is right about one thing, is she not?'

Flustered by his touch, all she could do was look at him and whisper softly, 'What?'

'That we are attracted to one another.' The rush of the waves was drowned out by the thudding of her heart. He'd admitted he found her attractive. 'If we act on that attraction, we can convince Xena our romance is real.'

Rio knew it wouldn't be that simple. This wasn't just a case of Xena feeling low after an accident had left her arm in plaster, unable to play the violin. When Xena's memory did return, she would be heartbroken all over again. Not just about her own romance with Ricardo but about Rio and Lysandros's, and knowing why Rio had broken it off, she would be devastated to think the accident, her amnesia had pushed Rio into such an arrangement.

'I really don't think Xena would believe us.' The pads of his thumbs caressed her hands, making her voice a husky whisper. He was holding her captive with the gentlest of touches, and while it unnerved her, she wanted to remain there, wanted his touch.

'Xena has already gone to great lengths to bring us together.' Lysandros's accent had deepened. 'She will believe us. It's what she wants most of all for us.'

'But what happens when she remembers we split up?' He was beginning to convince her, making her feel it could really work and, above all, making her wish it was all for real.

He smiled, one that showed such self-assurance it made her fingers clench tightly into her palms, digging her nails into the soft skin. 'I hope that we can return to where we were the afternoon of the recital.'

'I don't know that we can go back to that,' she said, still unbearably distracted by the caressing of his thumbs on her hands.

'You said you would do anything to help Xena with her amnesia.' His voice had become a seductive purr and she was unable to form any kind of reply as she looked into his eyes, seeing the same desire in them she'd seen when he'd last held her close. 'All we need to do is set free the sizzling desire between us. The desire we were so close to discovering, Rio.'

'That's gone.' She tried to inject strength into her declaration, but knew she'd failed.

'I disagree.' He touched her face and her breath shuddered in as the spark of desire she was desperate to deny ignited inside her. 'There is desire, Rio, and you can't hide from it for ever.'

CHAPTER THREE

LYSANDROS WATCHED AS desire chased the panic from Rio's eyes, their velvet brown becoming darker as her gaze held his. Around him, the sounds of the waves quietened. It was just the two of them. Nothing and no one else existed, and the heady tension, which had always been beneath the surface, began to take over.

Rio's full lips parted, and all he wanted was to kiss her, to taste the sweetness of her lips and forget the madness of recent days. He didn't want to think about Xena's amnesia, to worry it could be more than temporary. He wanted to lose himself in the passion he knew lived inside Rio. He wanted to set it free, convince her what they had was far too powerful to ignore. Or walk away from.

'I can't hide from what I don't feel.' Rio's words were husky and very sexy. So she still didn't dare admit it. His instinct was to kiss her, to prove to her she did feel desire. But he held back. There was an air of fragility about Rio, weaving in with the innocence in her eyes. He remembered what Xena had advised him after Rio had ended things. The need to give her time and space.

The rush of a bigger wave drew him from the bubble of isolation his thoughts had taken him to. He took her hand as she stepped towards him, avoiding the wave, and eased her gently closer to him. 'I don't believe that, Rio.'

She sighed, her lips pressing together as if she knew how utterly kissable she looked and was doing everything possible to avoid that. 'But I do,' she said firmly.

He searched her face, looking into her eyes, convinced the attraction was there, if only she would allow it to shine through. 'Is that really the truth?' He kept his voice calm and gentle, sensing she was more like a nervous foal who could bolt at the slightest thing.

She pulled her hand from his, stepping back from him as the undertow of water dragged another wave back out to sea, seeming to take her too. She looked lost. More vulnerable than he'd ever seen her, and he wished now he hadn't adhered to Xena's advice. He should have demanded to know why Rio had abruptly ended things between them. Because he needed to know. If only he'd asked Xena to explain what had happened to make Rio change her mind so quickly, so unexpectedly, after the recital.

Rio made him feel unsure of himself. He hadn't felt like that since Kyra's betrayal ten years ago. The effect Rio had had on him had been different, right from the day Xena had introduced them. The attraction had been instant, but Rio's innocent fragility had made him want to take things slowly. For the first time in many years he had wanted to build a relationship based on more than just sex. A fact Xena had been quick to pick up on, goading him in the way only a sister could about one day making things with Rio more permanent.

Then something had changed. Rio had changed, and Xena knew why. If only he had asked Xena then, instead of allowing his pride to keep him wrapped up in work in Athens. Now he couldn't do anything to risk upsetting the fragile state of his sister's memory and confidence. And it was for that very reason he and Rio needed to act as if they were still a couple, around Xena at least.

'Yes, it's true.' She stood there, the wet sand

gleaming in the sunlight around her, and she looked more beautiful than she'd ever looked. 'There is nothing between us, Lysandros. We should never have got together in the first place.'

He frowned at her, moving towards her as another wave rushed around his feet. 'Why is that, Rio?'

'We are too different.' Her explanation rushed at him faster than the waves were coming in, unbalancing him more than the undertow of water. The expression on her face left him in no doubt she believed that claim. He did not.

'If that is true, how did Xena manage to think we were so suited to one another?' As he spoke he realised the absurdity of the situation. His sister was the one person, apart from Rio herself, who could possibly tell him what had happened to make her change her mind. Yet Xena couldn't remember a thing about it. Not that he'd pressed her, not after the doctor's warning of not pushing her too hard too soon. But if Xena had blocked out all the bad events from her life in recent weeks and she still believed he and Rio were an item, there was only one conclusion he could draw. Whatever it was that had made Rio change her mind, it must have been bad. As upsetting for Xena as for Rio.

Rio smiled. A sad smile that held regret. 'Xena lives in a world of fantasy, where true love and happy-ever-afters exist. Surely you know that?'

He did. Only too well. His constant trips to London after he'd met Rio had certainly shown him that, as his sister had become convinced he and Rio had been on the path to one of those happy-ever-afters. He'd adopted the stance of ignoring her comments, hoping she'd find something new to focus on.

He nodded and smiled, wanting to lighten the mood, to put Rio at ease again. 'I do, yes. She has some very fixed ideas about us.'

'Except that she doesn't recall we are no longer dating,' Rio said, concern filling her voice. 'While I understand the doctors say she needs time to adjust to allow her memory to return and that it should be allowed to happen organically, I wish I could just tell her.'

'I don't think we should say anything yet.' Lysandros wasn't about to allow Rio to slip away from him so easily, not when he was finally beginning to break through her barriers. He looked at her, his gaze drawn to her lips, to the plump softness, and the urge to take her in his arms and kiss her rushed forward again. Maybe they should go back to the villa, back to Xena's company—before he lost the battle and kissed her.

'There you are.' Xena's voice cut through the tension in the warm air and Rio had never been so pleased to be interrupted. 'I should have known you two would be making the most of a bit of time alone.'

Rio smiled, but she was far from happy. Not only did Xena believe they were still dating, but Lysandros still wanted to know why she'd ended their relationship. She pushed her anxieties aside and walked towards Xena, relieved to move away from Lysandros. Away from the sensation that she was falling back under the intoxicating spell that was weaving around them again, just as it had the first day they'd met. She focused on Xena, trying to dismiss Lysandros from her thoughts. 'We thought we'd give you some peace to rest.'

'And we wanted a bit of time alone,' Lysandros said softly as he moved to her side, putting his arm around her, sending a rush of heat hurtling through her. His voice, filled with that lethal charm, always made her fall for him a little bit more. And now was no exception, but she couldn't afford to allow him to know that.

'What is it you shouldn't say to me?' Xena narrowed her eyes and pouted mischievously at Lysandros, and Rio held her breath. Would he tell Xena? Threaten the potential return of her memory by filling it with facts she needed to remember at her own pace?

'Did I say that?' Lysandros laughed and Rio felt the ice around her heart melt a little more as his genuine concern for Xena showed in his face. He might pretend to be the hard-edged businessman, but Xena could wrap him around her little finger in no time.

'Yes, Lysandros Drakakis. I distinctly heard you say, "I don't think we should say anything yet." What's it all about?'

'Isn't it time for us to be getting to your mother's?' Rio jumped into the conversation, trying to divert Xena's attention, but she just turned Xena's teasing suspicion on herself.

'You two are up to something.' Then her eyes widened and she looked at Lysandros, laughing. 'I wonder what it can be.'

'That's for me to know, little sister, not you,' Lysandros's voice teased as he turned Xena physically around, moving her back towards the villa. 'But right now it's time to go and see Mother.'

Rio began walking back to the villa as Xena continued to taunt Lysandros, but with that teasing now in Greek, Rio had little hope of understanding. Lysandros seemed to be denying whatever it was she was saying, but from the anxious look he cast at her as they entered the villa, Rio wondered just what had been said and what wild conclusions Xena had come to.

'Mother will be anxious to see you, Xena, and happy you are in such good spirits,' Lysandros said as he locked up the villa and they made their way to the jetty and his boat.

'She'll also be happy to see you two all loved up,' Xena taunted again, that look of mischief on her face getting ever stronger.

'We are not loved up,' Rio said quickly. Too quickly, if the warning look Lysandros shot her was anything to go by.

Xena laughed and teased Lysandros again in Greek. Whatever it was she was saying, it was making him distinctly uncomfortable. 'Stop fooling around,' he said lightly to Xena, and Rio was thankful he'd brought the conversation back to English. 'Mother will be waiting.'

After a short boat ride across the sea, they

arrived at the villa, and their mother, who must have been watching for them, hurried from her villa and down to the jetty. Rio hung back, wanting to give Xena a few moments alone with her mother. After enthusiastic hugs, Xena and her mother went inside, leaving Rio once again alone with Lysandros.

'Xena really seems excited,' Rio said as Lysandros secured the final rope on the boat. He looked up at her, the wind tousling his dark hair, and she curled her fingers tightly into the palms of her hands, trying to halt the thought of running them through his hair, for fear of giving in to that temptation.

'A bit too much perhaps.' He stood up and suddenly he was too close again.

He looked down at her, his expression serious and intense, and Rio's heart skipped a beat. Why did she still react like this to him? How could he still have that effect on her? He was slowly dismantling every barrier she'd put in place around herself, along with the extra defences she'd built up after Hans had tried to claim something from her she hadn't wanted to give.

She couldn't take her eyes from Lysandros, couldn't break the eye contact. Her body began to sway towards him and she bit at her bottom lip. She wanted to kiss him, wanted to go back to that moment after the recital when she'd promised him so much with just one kiss. But she couldn't. She wasn't ready for that. Not now. Not yet.

'We should go,' Lysandros said, his voice deep and firm, dragging her mind back from the past, back from what could never be again. He was angry with her. She could sense it. See it in the firm set of his shoulders as he looked at her. Guilt raced through her. She'd been ready to take their relationship further, ready to give him her virginity, and then she'd stood him up. She really did owe him an explanation. But where did she start? And with everything else going on with Xena—how?

Memories of Hans as he'd spoilt everything she could have had with Lysandros rushed at her. Any hopes for a future with Lysandros were still spoilt, unless she could talk to Lysandros, tell him what had happened that afternoon. But she wasn't ready to do that yet and she couldn't go back to where she and Lysandros had been. She would be so far out of her depth with him, she might as well be plunging into the sea. 'Yes, let's,' she said quickly. At least with Xena and his mother around, she would be safe. Safe from Lysandros and herself.

* * *

When they entered his mother's villa, Lysandros watched as she enveloped Rio in a big hug, welcoming her in stilted English. Did Rio's presence also make his mother believe they were back together? Or, worse, did his mother share Xena's hopes? That Rio was the woman he would finally settle down with?

Xena's teasing, which mercifully had been in Greek, left him in no doubt how his sister saw the situation between him and Rio. It was more worrying than her lack of memory. To Xena, Rio's presence in Greece was not simply to keep her company while she recovered from the accident. It wasn't even about his need to find out why he and Rio had broken up, not when Xena didn't recall that event. It was about his and Rio's future—together.

Xena believed wholeheartedly he was about to propose to Rio. A thought that filled Xena with much happiness. That, in itself, was shocking, but so too was the realisation that if he did propose it could help Xena, could help her to feel safe and secure and allow her memory to return.

'She is very beautiful.' His mother spoke in Greek as she came to stand beside him. He dragged himself from his thoughts and back to the moment, refusing to acknowledge the idea that was solidifying inside his mind.

He looked at Xena and Rio as they laughed and chatted together, their friendship clear. Rio was beautiful. And he still wanted her. 'She is,' he said softly.

'Don't lose her, Lysandros.' His mother's words jarred his mind and he jerked his head to look at her. She was under the same mis-apprehension as Xena. He could see the hope in her eyes.

'Lose Rio?' he questioned in Greek, aware the use of her name had caught Rio's attention. Xena, understanding the discussion with his mother, came to the rescue as she took Rio's arm, wanting to show her around the villa.

'You are perfect together,' his mother said as Rio and Xena left the room. 'It's time to put aside the past and settle down. Both Xena and I agree. Rio is perfect for you.'

He should be angry they had been talking, but he couldn't get the thought of having Rio back in his life out of his mind. It would give him the chance to find out what had happened to make her stand him up and what he could do to get back to the moment she'd kissed him, telling him he wanted to be his.

'You and Xena have been discussing us?' he

continued in Greek, aware that Rio and Xena could return at any moment.

'We have,' his mother said with a smile, along with a little embarrassment at being caught out. 'And if you and Rio are serious about one another, maybe now would be a good time to propose—for Xena's sake.'

He shook his head. Despite his earlier thoughts, he couldn't propose. Not when they weren't even dating. 'I don't have a ring.'

'There's Grandmother's.' Xena's voice startled him and he looked around for Rio. 'She'll be back in a moment. Oh, I can't wait to see you ask her.'

How the hell was he going to get out of this? Lysandros couldn't miss the joy on Xena's face, the excitement in her voice. If he told her she was wrong, told her he had no intention of proposing—to anyone—it might unbalance her when she least needed upset. He could hear again the doctor's words.

'Your sister's memory will return if she is happy and relaxed, but she doesn't need any emotional upset.'

'I will fetch it now,' his mother said, and Lysandros wanted to shout, no, wanted to tell her to stop. He didn't want to propose. A proposal would mean marriage. He didn't want to get engaged again, much less married. His mind whirred. But a temporary proposal, one to help Xena's recovery, would not have to lead to marriage…

It would give Xena something positive to focus on and maybe he and Rio could finally find time to deal with whatever it was that had made her run out on him. Maybe they could then share the passion of a night together? The night her last kiss had promised him?

'I have kept it all these years, sure that after Kyra you wouldn't want to shower a woman in shiny new diamonds again.' She clasped her hands in front of her chest, her eyes now sparkling with tears and excitement. 'Rio is the perfect girl to give the ring to.'

As his mother went to get the ring he rejoined Xena and Rio, who were chatting happily as if nothing untoward had ever happened, their bond of friendship clear to see. He briefly considered if the idea of a fake romance would work without this added pretence, but one look at Xena as she gave him a conspiratorial glance told him it was absolutely necessary to achieve his objective. She believed he was about to propose and anything less would upset her.

But what about Rio? Would she play along?

Would she do as she'd claimed and help Xena in any way she could?

Questions raced through his mind as his mother returned to the room, handing him a small box as she passed him, before she joined Rio and Xena. Rio looked apprehensive. She knew something was going on, but did she know he was about to up the stakes? Take everything to a level neither of them wanted?

He held the old and somewhat tatty box in his hand, knowing he was at a big turning point in his life. He was about to do the one thing he'd sworn he'd never do again. Ask a woman to marry him. He pushed the thought savagely aside, along with memories of the past. All he had to remember was that it wasn't real this time. It was easier to think of it as just an extra caveat in the deal between him and Rio to help his sister.

'I have something to ask, Rio,' he said, suddenly more anxious than he'd ever been in his life, not that he'd let anyone know. What the hell was wrong with him? He struck deals for shipping contracts and his new line of luxury yachts almost daily. Had faced all sorts of drama, yet he couldn't do this. Why?

Because you got it wrong once before.

Xena looked up at him, her expression anxious, making him wonder again what it was that was bothering her so much. 'Do it, Lysandros.'

He sensed Rio watching him as he held his sister's gaze. He could feel her scrutiny burning his skin, setting fire to the passion that had simmered dangerously close to the surface the last time he'd kissed her—just hours before she'd stood him up.

'Rio…' he began, turning to her, opening his hand to reveal the box his mother had just secretly given him. The squeal of delight Xena made as a hand flew to her lips fuelled his conviction that this was the right thing to do, and he moved closer to Rio, whose brows pulled together in confusion. 'Will you do me the honour of becoming my fiancée?'

The words came far more easily than he'd thought and he opened the box as Rio's eyes widened in shock. She looked down at the ring and then back at him, questions clearly running riot in her mind.

'But…' Her voice was barely a whisper and the whole room echoed with a heaviness of expectant silence.

Slowly he took her left hand, which shook, confirming she really was afraid of what he was doing. Carefully he slid the ring onto her finger. It was a perfect fit. She looked at him, the same shock he felt flooding her eyes. 'I want us to be engaged.'

CHAPTER FOUR

'I…' RIO BEGAN, stumbling over her words.

Lysandros's fingers tightened on hers, and the soft and caring expression in his eyes, which she wasn't going to allow herself to be fooled by, intensified. She forced out her words as her heart thumped and adrenaline raced through her. 'It's an engagement ring.'

'And I want you to wear it.' Lysandros's voice was deep, full of charm. If he was trying to win her round, he was almost succeeding. This was what she'd secretly wished for once, before…

Xena squealed again and Rio looked at her friend. She was ecstatic. 'This is perfect,' Xena said, clapping her hands together despite the cast on her wrist. 'It's exactly what I've always hoped for.'

Rio's heart sank. She was trapped. Not only by the expectant look on Lysandros's hand-

some face but by Xena's—and even their
mother's—excitement. If she turned Lysandros down, said no, wouldn't it upset Xena?
Stress her in a way the doctor had warned
against doing?

But if she said yes? She would be engaged
to Lysandros. It would be more than just acting as if they were still dating. Far more. Could
she really do that? For Xena? Could she become engaged to Lysandros, the man she'd
once wanted—and still did, if she was truly
honest with herself? Could she say yes? Just
for now?

She looked at Lysandros. Did he really mean
it or was he doing this for Xena? Had he also
realised his sister had high hopes for them as a
couple? Her throat felt tight, as if she couldn't
speak, and she pressed her lips together, desperate to keep the answer she was considering—purely for Xena's benefit.

Rio was acutely aware of Xena's building
excitement—of her happiness. Had Lysandros
planned to do this all along? Even at the hospital? Was that why he'd been so insistent she go
to Greece with Xena? He could have warned
her. Could have discussed it with her. Anger
simmered through her and she looked into his
eyes, desperate to find some way out, a way

to say no that wouldn't plunge Xena back into misery. But there wasn't one. Not now he'd done this.

'Rio?' Lysandros questioned softly. So softly it was as if he really did care. 'Say something.'

He drew her closer, still holding her hand, the heat of his touch scalding her. His increasing nearness made rational thought almost impossible as, despite everything, tingles of awareness sparked over her.

'I don't know what to say.'

'Yes, of course you know,' Xena burst out. 'You say yes.'

'That would be the preferred option.' Even though Lysandros was smiling and his touch on her fingers was light and gentle, there was a gleam of determination in his dark eyes and she knew there was only one answer he wanted her to give.

'I don't know.' Could she really do this? Become engaged, even as part of a sudden plan to help Xena? Could she say yes to the man she'd never believed would become her fiancé? It was such a cruel twist of fate after all she'd been through.

'Rio, you have to say yes,' Xena said, her words finally breaking through Rio's thoughts. The roller coaster Rio was hurtling along on

was getting faster and scarier with each passing second. She wanted it to stop. Wanted to
get off. 'You and Lysandros are made for each
other and planning an engagement party *and
then* a wedding will be so much fun. Maybe
it will even help me remember again.'

Rio looked back up at Lysandros, her heart
pounding as nerves surged through her. Then
he smiled. A smile that had self-satisfaction
stamped all over it. Damn the man. He knew
she wouldn't be able to refuse Xena. He knew
he'd won. Got what he wanted.

'What do you think, Rio?' He brushed her
hair from her face in a caring and loving gesture, forcing Rio to fight against the flurry
of butterflies in her tummy. Xena cooed over
the gesture. 'Shall we get engaged? Give Xena
something that could help her remember?'

'How can I not say yes?' She forced a happy
smile to her face as his gaze held hers, hoping
he noticed the annoyance in her eyes. Behind
her, she was aware of his mother and Xena
talking rapidly in Greek. Probably already
making plans, if she knew Xena.

'That is exactly what I'd hoped you would
say.' Was that relief as his shoulders visibly
relaxed? Had he thought she'd go back on the

one thing she'd agreed to—anything to help his sister?

Rio dragged in a ragged deep breath. The look in his eyes, the intensity and desire, almost fooled her that this moment was real. That he loved her, wanted her in his life. Xena jumped for joy like a kitten after twine, hugging her mother, making her realise it *was* real. But not in the way it should be. She might have just agreed to an engagement with a man she had once loved, but she knew he didn't want commitment. That this wasn't in any way real for him. Now, more than ever, she had to guard her heart, protect herself and bury all she'd once felt for him.

'We need champagne,' Xena said as she came and hugged Rio before turning to her mother. 'Let's go and find some. Leave these two alone for a moment.'

'I can't believe you just did that.' Rio's shocked words were little more than a whisper as she watched his mother and Xena leaving, talking rapidly in Greek. What had just happened? The roller coaster she desperately wanted to get off looped violently. She touched the ring on her left hand. She was engaged. To Lysandros.

'You heard Xena. It will give her something

to focus on, maybe even help her regain her memory.' Lysandros spoke softly and quietly, standing far too close. Her heart raced, and even though her head was warning caution, her body began responding to that nearness in a way that terrified and excited her. He'd decided how this fake engagement was going to play out and that was that. She had no choice but to go with it or risk Xena's chance of recovering her memory.

She looked into his eyes, the darkness full of warmth, and her stomach, along with her heart, flipped over. Was he doing this, making her feel like this, purposely? She refused to think about that, refused to be anything but detached from this whole situation. She couldn't let her heart get involved in his scheme. All she had to do was go along with it for now, string the engagement out for as long as possible and, above all, remember she was doing this for Xena.

'Champagne,' Xena called, as she returned carrying a bottle, her mother following with a tray of glasses.

'Perfect,' Rio said, trying to put some enthusiasm into her voice, trying to make this whole charade seem real. For her sake as much as Xena's.

'Now we really do have something to celebrate. I'm going to be busy planning an engagement party.' The pitch of Xena's voice rose to a crescendo in her excitement and for some bizarre reason Rio found this amusing and laughed. The whole situation was so far removed from reality it didn't seem possible.

Lysandros let go of her hand, putting his arm around her, drawing her even closer to him. The shock of his body against hers silenced the laughter, probably exactly the effect he'd wanted. 'There will be no need for fuss. Rio and I only want to celebrate our engagement with those closest to us.'

The reality of what she was doing finally filtered through like a mountain stream over the rocks. 'Nothing big.' Rio began to realise the implications of their engagement. It would be almost as binding as marriage.

'Only a small family gathering,' reassured his mother as she patted Rio's arm gently, a big smile on her face and happiness sparkling in her eyes. 'Here on the island.'

Rio's heart sank. Yet more guilt to carry. Had Lysandros even thought this through? The pretence of an engagement was a lie that had far-reaching effects. The happiness on his mother's face already chastised her, ratcheting up her guilt.

'My mother will ensure Xena doesn't get carried away while we are away.' Lysandros turned her to face him, lifting her chin upwards with his thumb and forefinger. A gesture that was so intimate all she could do was swallow down her nerves.

'Away?' Panic raced through her.

'Now I have officially proposed, we can spend some time together, making up for the weeks we have been apart.'

Rio's cheeks burned with embarrassment at what he was insinuating. Did he have no shame? To say such things in front of his mother and sister? She nodded, unable to break eye contact with him, becoming more unaware of what was going on around her with every passing second. As if they were already totally alone.

'That would be perfect,' she said softly, looking into his eyes, playing the role of adoring fiancée to the full. She might well be dragging them further into this charade, but she wanted him to feel the same way she had when he'd sprung his proposal on her.

'My yacht is ready to leave immediately. We will spend the weekend together.' He smiled at her, his thumb lightly brushing to and fro on her chin, causing sensations she had no right to be feeling.

'How romantic,' said Xena with a sigh, reminding them both they were certainly not alone right now. 'I *always* knew you two would be perfect for one another.'

Lysandros laughed. A deep sexy sound, adding to her current torture, and she was thankful for Xena's interruption, for the reminder they weren't alone, that this wasn't real. 'In that case, you would have no objection to me whisking my brand-new fiancée away right now.'

'Just go.' Xena laughed, the sound so light and carefree, so like the girl she'd been before the accident, it intensified Rio's guilt, adding weight to Lysandros's unspoken argument that getting engaged—temporarily—was the right thing to do. For Xena at least.

Lysandros took Rio's hand in his once more and led her away from the villa. Away from his mother and sister's scrutiny. He wrapped his hand tightly around hers, taking a deep breath as he felt the stone of the engagement ring pressing into his fingers. The shock at what he'd just done combined with a slowly in-

tensifying desire for a woman who had turned
him down, forming a heady cocktail.

'Xena looked pleased.' Rio's voice was hard
and accusing, dousing the rising desire in him.
He let her hand go, unable to bear the warmth
of her skin on his, heightening his body's response to her.

'You told me you'd do anything to help
Xena.' He couldn't keep the irritation from
his voice, the growl reminiscent of one of
the island's many wild cats when cornered.
And right now that was exactly how he felt.
Cornered by the hope in his mother's eyes.
Cornered by Xena's excitement. But like any
animal in that situation, he refused to show
his weakness or his doubt. He had to remain
strong and in control.

He could still see his sister, smiling. Could
still see his mother, hope lighting her eyes,
leaving him in no doubt she expected so much
from him, from the marriage proposal. He saw
again Rio looking up at him, the unspoken attraction between them clear in her eyes, felt the
powerful passion she could so easily induce. He
had to remember why they were really doing
this, and that it was the right thing to do. Already there was a big difference in Xena.

'You took the idea of a fake relationship to

a completely different level.' She hurled the words at him as they made their way to his speedboat, which would take them to his yacht anchored at sea. 'You're the one who suggested we stage a romance, and then, if that wasn't enough, you took the elaborate charade one step further by proposing.' She glared at him. 'What was that all about?'

Her voice had risen with each word, anger mixing with panic in her eyes as she turned to look at him. The sudden urge to pull her against him was too intense. He wanted to hold her tightly, kiss her until every drop of anger melted into the sort of passion he knew she would be capable of. Her outward appearance of innocence didn't fool him. Beneath that indifferent exterior was a passionate woman. He'd tasted it in her kiss after the recital.

'What was it all about?' He threw her question back at her, fighting hard to ignore his increasing need for her, drawing instead on exasperation that she was unaware of what he'd been doing. 'It was all about making our relationship convincing.'

'Convincing?' Anger slipped quickly from her voice, which had become a husky whisper of confusion.

She was giving in. He was going to get exactly what he wanted out of this arrangement. Their engagement had become far more than not stressing his sister. He now had Rio to himself and could finally get to the bottom of why she'd abruptly ended their relationship. A relationship that, despite not getting further than passionate kisses, had held the promise in each and every one of so much more, and not just physically. For the first time since Kyra, he'd wanted that.

'What happens when we split up? Because we can't remain engaged. What is Xena going to do then?' Rio's harsh words struck a chord. 'Or worse, what happens when she regains her memory?'

The image of his mother's face and the hope in her eyes flashed before him, reminding him of the one thing, as the only son, he had failed her in—settling down and having a family.

'I assume your reckless plan involves us splitting up as soon as that happens?'

'When the time is right, we will do exactly that.' That time would be once he'd found out everything he needed to know. In the meantime he'd enjoy being in Rio's company.

'I still can't believe you did that—and without a word of warning to me.'

'Engagement is the only way to convince Xena this is real.'

'But engagement?' she blurted out. 'That's so final. So permanent.'

'Not as permanent as marriage.' The truth of that hit him as he looked into Rio's eyes. 'Think of this engagement as a deal.'

'A deal?' Her eyes widened in shock. 'And what will this deal entail?'

'We will allow Xena to plan an engagement party, but once Xena's memory returns, we can call off the deal, end the engagement. Unless you can fill in the blanks for Xena—and me?'

She gasped and looked at him, her brows pulling together in an angry line. 'You are ruthless.'

She turned from him as if she was about to walk away. 'Yes, I am, Rio, and I always get what I want.' And right now he wanted her.

She swung back to face him. 'Is this really the way to help Xena?'

'It is the only way to help Xena. You and I will be engaged and we will remain so for as long as it takes for Xena to regain her health.'

'Then what?' she snapped at him.

'Then you can return to England.'

'You are quite something, Lysandros Drakakis.' The disbelief in her voice chipped at his conscience, dented his protective armour, re-kindling the emotions she'd stirred in him before ending things between them.

'Your compliment is well received,' he taunted her, liking the flush of anger on her pale cheeks.

'What happens when Xena expects us to get married, when she—?' she began, but he cut across her before she had any notions of anything else.

'As I have just said, it's to help Xena. Once her memory has returned there will be no need for such a course of action. We can simply call off the engagement.'

She inhaled deeply as if trying to calm herself, and he smothered a smile of amusement. She certainly had hidden fire within her. 'And what will we do while we are engaged to make it convincing?'

'Give the outward appearance of a couple in love—madly and passionately in love.'

The sound of the clear waters of the sea against his boat as they stood on the jetty infiltrated his thoughts. He looked beyond Rio, to his mother's villa in the distance, and saw Xena and his mother standing on the terrace. He looked back at Rio.

'Xena and my mother are watching us right

now, so if you meant what you said in the hospital, that you would do anything to help Xena, even make her believe our engagement is real, you will now put your arms around my neck and kiss me.'

'I will do no such thing.'

'Does that mean you lied to me, Rio?' He moved a little closer, so that Xena and his mother would think it an intimate gesture. Heated desire surged through him, catching him off guard. Just being that close to her was a temptation, making his voice fiercer than he intended. 'I don't like lies, Rio.'

If he wasn't mistaken, she actually gulped. Had she been lying? And if so, what else was she lying about?

'We don't need to go that far. We don't need to kiss.' Her voice wavered but his determination to do the right thing for his sister didn't.

'This is a deal, Rio, a deal between the two of us to help Xena overcome the effects of the accident. All you need to do is play out a romantic engagement, act the part of being in love and kiss me.'

She shook her head slowly, but her eyes still held his, her full lips parted slightly, igniting his desire once more. 'You really expect me to kiss you? Now? Here?'

'Neither Xena or my mother will be convinced by anything less than seeing us not only engaged but as lovers.'

Rio paled so rapidly he wondered if she was going to pass out. 'I can't believe I've agreed to this.'

'Think of it as sealing our contract.' He kept his voice low and gentle, her resistance beginning to dwindle. 'Remember how happy Xena was just now. All we need to do is provide the illusion of romance between us—for a couple of weeks at least.'

'I can't kiss you.' Her voice was a breathy whisper, sending shivers of passion all over him.

'You've kissed me before,' he said, watching the turmoil in her eyes. 'Do you really dislike me that much now?'

'Don't.' She looked down and he wanted to lift her chin, make her look at him, make her see the desire in his eyes.

'Kiss me, Rio.' His voice had become a hoarse whisper. 'The desire hasn't gone away, has it?'

'No, but things have changed.' She looked up at him, urgency in her gaze. 'I've changed.'

'Then perhaps you should tell me.' He brushed his fingers over her cheek, wanting to understand, wanting to know.

She shook her head rapidly. 'I can't—not yet.'

'But you will tell me? Soon?' he whispered, trying to keep the annoyance from his voice. Yet again she was backing out of giving him the answers he needed. Patience was what he needed—and charm. He'd seduce the answers from her, slowly and subtly.

She nodded and looked up at him. 'I will, Lysandros, I promise.'

'Then for now I will wait. Time alone will help. A long romantic weekend on my yacht to relax with one another will be just that. It's also the sort of thing Xena would expect me to do and will reinforce our engagement.'

'I'm not sure,' Rio said huskily, and he knew he was getting to her.

'I am.' He smiled down at her, saw her lips part, heard the ragged breath she drew in.

'What will happen afterwards? When we come back?'

'You want to spend more time with me, *agape mou*?' Her eyes widened in shock as she realised where she'd inadvertently led the conversation.

'That's not what I meant.' The defensiveness of her tone couldn't hide her confusion—or the attraction she was clearly fighting.

'I will spend most of my time working in

Athens and you will be here with Xena.' He tried to put her mind at rest as well as tell himself what would happen. It was far more than having work to do; it was putting the temptation she aroused in him out of his reach. Give her the space Xena had told him she wanted, the distance he sensed she still needed.

'That's it? Nothing more?'

He smiled, using the charm he was renowned for. 'Xena and Mother are still there, still watching.' She frowned up at him, her lips pouting in an inviting way. 'Step into my embrace, Rio, and kiss me.'

Rio's eyes widened with shock and she stayed very still for a few seconds. She wasn't going to provide the evidence of being in love, the kiss that would seal their deal and convince his sister and mother.

'Kiss me, Rio.'

She hesitated then slowly moved towards him. He put his arms around her, holding her gently at her lower back as she put her arms up around the back of his neck, her sun hat dangling loosely from one hand on his back.

Lust leapt to life within him as he brought her body against his, the shock on her face leaving him in no doubt she'd felt it too. Her breathing was deep and slow as they moved closer, bodies pressing together, her eyes darkening and locking with his.

Seconds later he claimed her lips, the sweetness of them almost taking his breath away. He tightened his hold on her, pulling her closer, giving himself up to the intensity of the kiss. Rio murmured with pleasure and he kissed her harder, deeper, slipping his tongue into her mouth, demanding so much more from her. Passion exploded, and he forgot it was meant to be part of an act. Desire crashed over him, reminding him, if he'd needed it, how much he wanted Rio.

Without thought for anything else, his hands slid down her back to the curve of her bottom. Her arms tightened around his neck as he moulded her against the hardness of his erection. She groaned with pleasure, making him even harder as she moved against him, tormenting and exciting him.

Being temporarily engaged to this woman was not going to be a hardship at all.

Rio could hardly breathe and certainly couldn't think as hot pleasure rushed all around her, awakening the woman within her. The fear of being kissed by a man, of being held close against his body after Hans had tried to force himself on her, was swept aside by raw desire.

But wasn't that dangerous?

She shouldn't want to allow herself the pleasure of Lysandros's kiss, or the sensation of sparks of desire shooting around her as she felt the evidence of his need for her. She shouldn't want more than the kiss, but the desire was too powerful to resist. He was too powerful to resist.

He pulled back from her, whispering against her lips, intensifying the surge of pleasure pulsing through her so wildly. 'A kiss such as that would convince even me that you still desired me.'

'I was doing it for Xena.' She pushed herself away from the temptation of kissing him again, of giving in to the pleasure of his caresses, of needing to feel his body pressed erotically against her.

He laughed. A sound so sexy she shivered. 'Then I do after all believe you. You will do anything for Xena.'

'I meant it,' she said, stepping back from him, disengaging her heated body from his, acutely aware of the danger he presented to her uninitiated body. She needed to be far more careful. She *had* to resist his potent charms, his seductive caresses and his passionate kisses.

'In that case, we will return to Xena's villa so that you may pack for our *romantic* weekend aboard my yacht.'

'We are leaving straight away?' Did he really mean to whisk her off right now? How could she spend any more time in his company when she'd just reacted like that to his kiss?

'What about Xena?'

'She and my mother have much planning to do while we are away spending time alone—keeping up the pretence of being in love.'

That determined and powerful authority had returned to his voice. At least that was easier to deal with. It was far more preferable, leaving her with more control than the hard-to-resist seduction he'd just proved he was more than capable of—and which she'd proved she was far from able to resist.

CHAPTER FIVE

THE GENTLE ROCKING of the yacht had drawn Rio from her sleep. Sleep that had been hard to find the previous night with her body still humming with the need that kiss outside his mother's villa had evoked. A need that had only intensified during the evening as she and Lysandros had dined aboard his yacht. Every time his eyes had met hers, she'd seen the flames licking higher, making the air crackle with sexual tension, making her want to be kissed again.

The warm evening air had been heavy with desire and it had scared Rio. Scared her because she'd wanted to act on it, wanted to take herself back to the moment after the recital when she'd teasingly asked Lysandros to take her to dinner, to spend the entire night with her.

She'd wanted that same thing last night. Had wanted it so much but was thankful that, despite the desire in every look he'd given her, he hadn't acted on it. He hadn't tried to touch her in any way. When Lysandros had insisted she take the large and luxurious master cabin alone, she'd been grateful. He'd saved her from herself and as soon as she'd shut the door she'd locked it, not against Lysandros but against the urge to go back to him and allow the passion between them to ignite—fully and completely.

He was so powerful, so dominating. She wasn't ready to let go of her fears and be intimate with him, despite the burning need for him. The decision to spend a night with him after the recital had taken weeks to come to and Hans's attempt on her had taken her so far backwards she needed to start again. She couldn't allow herself to be carried away by a heady kiss. She needed to find again the woman who'd seductively kissed Lysandros that afternoon at the recital.

That would take time to rediscover and, no matter how charming Lysandros was, she couldn't do anything until she was completely ready.

'Rio?' As if conjured up by her imagination, Lysandros's voice sounded from the other side of the door, making her heart pound erratically.

She opened the cabin door, looking into his handsome face. Her breath caught at the image he created as he stood there dressed more casually than she'd ever seen him but looking just as lethal as he did in his designer suit. The effect he had on her was so profound she couldn't say anything.

'I have arranged a special breakfast for us as we are supposed to be newly engaged lovers.' His dark eyes held a hint of mischief, a smile playing around his lips. Was that why he seemed more devastatingly handsome, more charming than normal, because he was smiling instead of betraying the hard-edged businessman she knew he really was? Was the smile and charm part of the act? Of course it was. She chastised herself for thinking otherwise.

'Very thorough.' Rio finally found her voice and joined in with the game he was playing, wondering what his crew thought about their separate sleeping arrangements. It certainly wouldn't look like they were lovers, and as he must have brought so many women to his yacht, she was sure they'd never occupied separate beds. 'But won't it have undermined your engagement plan as we spent the night apart?'

'Are you saying you would rather share my bed?' A wicked grin slipped over his face, sending her pulse rate soaring, setting her cheeks on fire.

'No,' she said quickly. Too quickly, if the look on his face was anything to go by. She blushed, remembering how he'd made her feel last night. How she'd wanted nothing more than to share his bed. 'But I'm sure it's not what you normally do when you have female guests aboard.'

'True.' He stepped closer, the spark in his eyes leaving her in no doubt the desire for her was still there and that he was enjoying her embarrassment. 'You are my fiancée and, as far as anyone else is concerned, we are waiting until we are married to share a bed, are we not?'

'N-no one will b-believe that.' She stammered over her response as an image of her sharing a bed with this handsome Greek filled her mind. She couldn't allow herself to imagine such things. 'Not when you are known for being such a…' She struggled for the right word.

'Playboy?' he offered, amusement mixing deliciously with his seductive voice. 'You, *agape mou*, have stolen my heart, made me turn my back on my bachelor playboy ways. What is so unbelievable about that?'

'I doubt many people will believe *I've* made you change.' She had to keep him at a distance, had to stop this light flirting. She wasn't the same woman who'd once been ready to give him her virginity, her love. 'What matters is that Xena believes it. I don't really care what anyone else thinks.'

He had the nerve to laugh at her and that sexy laughter almost unleashed the desire she was so determined to keep hidden. As if sensing her turmoil, he smiled at her, setting free his lethal charm. 'Breakfast, *agape mou*? A romantic breakfast for lovers?'

Could she do this? Act as if they were lovers? A newly engaged and happy couple? It had been everything she'd secretly wanted—once. She wasn't at all sure she could keep her heart from being broken, but she had to do this. For Xena. If it wasn't for the accident having wiped out Xena's memory, she wouldn't even be in Greece, let alone on this yacht with Lysandros. Whatever else she did, she had to remember that. 'Fine. I will be ready in five minutes.'

She used those five minutes to steady her heartbeat and compose herself. She needed to maintain a prickly hostility towards him, bury the attraction she was fighting. He had to believe there wasn't or couldn't be anything between them. It was the only way to keep her heart unscathed and play the role of temporary fiancée.

She picked up her sunglasses and sun hat and with renewed determination left the safety of the cabin. The sheer luxury of the yacht still amazed her as she walked up onto the deck. She recalled Xena's pride that he'd turned an ordinary shipping business into one that supplied the rich and famous all around the world with luxury yachts, and being here, in this almost fantasy setting, she could understand how it had become so successful.

'You look very beautiful.' The soft seductive purr of his voice as he took her hand, guiding her towards the stern of the yacht, sent a flurry of butterflies all through her. He was taking the role of a man in love with his fiancée very seriously, playing it out to perfection. How she longed for it to be real, to be able to go back to the recital and never leave to meet Hans, never go through that life-changing moment.

'You mentioned breakfast?' The teasing note in her voice was so unlike her that she couldn't help but blush. What was she doing, flirting with him? None of this was real. His proposal. Even the beautiful ring she wore. It was merely a temporary arrangement, one he'd already decided would end the moment Xena recovered her memory.

Yet despite knowing this, her attraction to him was getting stronger each day. She was in danger of losing herself, her heart to him. But she couldn't do that, not when she had no idea how he would react if he knew why she'd stood him up, why she'd ended their relationship so abruptly. He was a man who'd avoided all emotional involvement, so surely wouldn't want to deal with that kind of revelation, not when she'd need his support, his strength to make it.

She couldn't look at him, but the gentleness of his voice calmed her. 'I did. This way.'

He led her down the steps to the platform at the end of the yacht, climbing into the small boat and turning to look up at her. She hid her confusion over her emotions behind a question. 'Where are we going?'

He quirked a brow at her as she finally found the courage to look into his handsome face. That sexy devil-may-care smile tugged at the attraction she was desperately trying to ignore. 'Breakfast awaits.'

With his help, she stepped into the small boat, the motion of it unsteadying her, but not as much as Lysandros did as he held her arms, drawing her close to him. She looked up at him, that spark it was so crucial to ignore zapping between them, stronger than the sunshine sparkling on the sea around them.

'I wasn't expecting that,' she said, her voice far too husky for her liking. She couldn't do anything other than look into his eyes.

'Neither was I.' His eyes, dark and heavy with the same kind of desire she'd seen yesterday in the moments after they'd kissed, pierced into her soul. Her breath caught audibly and she bit her teeth into her bottom lip.

'I meant the wobble of the boat,' she quickly defended herself, but from his slow smile he was as aware of that desire as she was—and how it had made her feel.

The temptation to slide his fingers into Rio's hair, to brush them against the softness of her cheeks and taste the sweetness of her lips, as he had done yesterday, was almost impossible to resist. The memory of that kiss still burned on Lysandros's lips, and the heady desire, which had rampaged through him as he'd held her against him, surged forward again.

That kiss should prove to Rio they were good together. For him, it had rekindled all the desire for her he'd been keeping in check on each date they'd enjoyed. It had brought it all back. Stronger than ever—and harder to resist.

'Then we had better get to shore.' He focused his mind on the task at hand instead of the memory of how she'd felt in his arms, against his body.

'Yes, I think that would be a good idea.' Her voice remained husky as she moved away from him, sitting down in the boat. He turned his attention to starting the motor and getting them to the beach. At least that was a normality that would take his mind off how she made him feel.

As the little boat moved quickly across the water Lysandros watched Rio, taking in her long, slender, tanned legs, still bemused by the fact that she'd chosen white shorts and a loose-fitting red-and-white-striped blouse. Any other woman he'd spent time on his yacht with would have emerged clad in the skimpiest of bikinis, even at the beginning of the day. It seemed that Rio wanted to conceal herself, but that didn't prevent him imagining her in a bikini.

'Here we are,' he said as the small boat pulled alongside the purpose-built jetty at the end of the beach, fighting the surge of heated lust as that image burned in his mind.

'This looks very secluded.' She stepped out onto the jetty, looking around the small sandy cove, appearing in awe of her surroundings. 'And very beautiful.'

'This is the perfect beach on which to have breakfast.' It was also a beach he'd never taken another woman to, and for reasons he couldn't yet fathom, that felt right. Everything about being with Rio was uncharted waters and he wanted this weekend to be the same.

For a moment she held his gaze, questions showing in her eyes, obliterating any of the desire he thought he'd seen earlier. Was she suddenly nervous of being here with him? Was the thought of being alone with him too much?

He sensed the need to tread carefully around her. If he was ever going to find out why Rio had abruptly changed her mind about dating him, he needed to be even more patient and gentle than before.

He still didn't understand it. One minute she'd been alive with joy at the recital, flirting playfully with him, letting him know she was ready to take their relationship further. Ready to be his—all night. Then it had all changed.

What had happened after she'd left him to meet the conductor? What had happened to make her stand him up? No message. Nothing. He'd never been stood up before and had tried to call Xena, not knowing how to deal with it. But Xena hadn't known—at least, not that night.

He needed to know why, what she felt for him, then and now. For some reason, one he wasn't yet ready to explore, it mattered to him what Rio thought. He wanted to reassure her that the undeniable attraction that hummed in the air around them whenever they were together was right on so many levels.

'My goodness,' she gasped in surprise as she saw the picnic laid out ready for them. 'When did you do all this?'

'A member of my crew set this up a short while ago.' That was the kind of reaction he'd hoped for when he'd planned this romantic picnic breakfast on a deserted beach.

She looked around the beach as if searching for that crew member. She was afraid to be alone with him. Was it because she didn't trust him or because she didn't trust herself? Was the attraction he was certain she felt for him the same attraction he felt for her, too strong to resist?

'And this is a private beach?' There was a definite tremor in her voice, a clear hint of anxiety.

'I had the distinct impression you would rather our romance and engagement were played out as little as possible in the public eye, so coming here like this seemed the perfect solution.' His motivation for this had been so far from that and guilt stabbed at him. All he'd wanted had been to resume where the kiss had ended yesterday. Take it to the passionate conclusion it had promised.

'Thank you.' Her voice was throaty and incredibly sexy.

He sat on the edge of the white blanket that had been spread out in readiness for them, opening the picnic basket, taking out waffles, fruit and the flowers he'd requested. Rio stood for a second, watching, before kneeling on the blanket. He could sense her suspicion, feel her wary gaze on him.

'We will, however, have to be seen out together at least once before our engagement party.'

'Seen out?' She looked at him sharply. The pleasure at the picnic he'd arranged had diminished the reality of their situation, but she must realise that while she played the role of his fiancée, she would be expected to be at his side when he attended important functions. Especially the charity ball in Athens. It was a charity he'd started and Xena would ask questions if Rio didn't go. He'd always had a beautiful woman on his arm at such events. This time it would be Rio. His temporary fiancée.

'It's an annual event I always attend. A charity close to my heart. Xena and most definitely my mother would find it strange if you didn't accompany me.'

'Surely it would be better if I stayed with Xena? After all, that's why I came, to keep her company, help her recover.' There was an element of pleading in her voice, but he refused to be drawn by it.

He might have used Xena as the reason to bring Rio to Greece, but if he was completely honest, it had been for his own reasons. He'd always found it difficult to let anyone emotionally close and Kyra's deceit had only intensified that. From the moment he and Rio had met, she'd had a strange power over him. She'd begun to prise open the door to his emotions. A door he'd slammed shut after Kyra's rejection. But Rio was changing that, and he'd refused to accept they were over. Not when there had been so much desire simmering around them. She made him feel and he wanted that, wanted to open himself to her, to connect on a level he'd blocked out for so long.

He poured the coffee, allowing the strong aroma to sharpen his senses. 'You are a true friend to Xena, doing all you can to help her recover.' He didn't miss the slight lift of her delicate brows. He hadn't been referring to their engagement deal, but she'd taken it that way.

'You didn't leave me much choice, Lysandros,' she berated him, swiftly taking the opportunity he'd unwittingly created to let him know her true thoughts. 'Even in the hospital you made me feel I wasn't a good friend if I didn't agree to your suggestions.'

The annoyance in her face was clear and he tried to soothe her ruffled mood. 'Xena is happy, settled. Everything the doctor said she needed to be to get over her amnesia. I hope that happens soon. I don't like seeing her like this.'

Rio changed position, going from kneeling to curling her legs at one side, and she couldn't look him in the eyes. 'I hope so too.' She looked down, her attention intensely focused on the picnic before her, which they had both forgotten. He leant closer, needing to look into her face, to see the expression her beauty could so easily mask.

She still didn't look at him, still focusing

all her attention on the picnic as if it were a lifeline.

'I want Xena to get better as much as you do. Why do you think we are doing this?' He paused, allowing the soft rush of the waves onto the beach to fill the silence.

'But now we are engaged.' She looked into his eyes, the passion of her words taking him aback.

'An engagement that will end as soon as Xena's memory returns.' He held her gaze, watched as her eyes darkened and, just as they had yesterday, her lips parted invitingly. 'Is being engaged to me really so bad?'

'No.' Her soft whisper spurred him on. 'There was a time when…'

Her words trailed off, taking him back to that afternoon in London. Back to the recital, the kiss that had left her glowing with desire. How could that have changed so swiftly?

'What happened, Rio? Why didn't you meet me that evening?'

Rio shook her head, refusing to say anything. He sensed he was closer to discovering why and he needed to know. This was more than just wounded male pride.

'Did you regret saying you wanted to spend the night with me? Did you change your mind?'

Rio looked at him as if she was considering her answer, as if she was trying to find a way to not admit what she really wanted to admit.

'It wouldn't have mattered if you had,' he continued when she didn't answer. 'I'm not in the habit of forcing myself on a woman.'

Her eyes widened, and she dragged in a long, deep breath. Did she really believe that he was like that? He touched her hand gently. 'Rio?'

'Yes. I changed my mind.' There was so much sadness, so much emotion in that answer that for a moment he couldn't say anything, the sound of the sea enveloping them.

'Why, Rio?' Eventually he found the words. 'Why, when you seemed so happy?'

He frowned. Why was she holding out on him? Suspicion and fury blended together. He looked at Rio as large tears sprang from her eyes and began to roll down her cheeks.

'Rio.' Shocked by the wave of protectiveness that had surged over him, he moved to take her in his arms and offer comfort.

She curled into him, her cheek pressing against his chest as he knelt next to her. She shuddered, fighting for control, and instinctively he pressed his lips against the top of her head. The fresh scent of her shampoo invaded his senses. Heated memories erupted, reminding him of the desire just kissing her could evoke. Even a compassionate kiss like that.

He looked up at the blue sky, the heat of the sun warming his face. As he looked back down, Rio pulled slightly away from him, looking up. Her eyes, still heavy with tears, searched his, and all he could think about was kissing her and making her sadness go away.

He lowered his head and moved closer, so close he was almost touching her face, almost kissing her. With a force that shocked him she pushed away from him.

'I can't do this.' She leapt to her feet, her breathing hard and fast. 'I can't kiss you again. I don't want to.'

She turned and walked away from him, stumbling as she hurried towards the jetty and the boat he'd tied up there not so very long ago.

'Rio. Wait.' He hurried after her, bemused by her sudden change of mood. She'd looked like she'd wanted to kiss him. Her lips had parted, waiting for his to claim them. Then her mood had changed, drastically and quickly, because he'd tried to kiss her. He'd done almost the exact thing he'd just claimed he wasn't in the habit of doing.

He caught up with her, grasping her hand, pulling her to a stop, needing her to look at him. When she did the wildness, the fear in her eyes shocked him.

'I should never have come to Greece. I should never have agreed to this, any of it. I can't do it, Lysandros. I just can't.'

He had to know what this was about. 'When you kissed me at the recital, it was a kiss of passion, full of meaning. It was there yesterday too, Rio. What exactly is it you're scared of? Me?'

She tried to pull her hand free of his, but he didn't want to let her go. He wanted to hold her closer still, keep her safe from whatever it was she feared.

'Yes.' She fired the word at him faster than a bullet from a gun. 'I'm scared of you, so just let me go.'

'Scared of me?' He couldn't help the incredulous tone of his voice as anger and confusion mixed together, making a potent cocktail.

He saw the same fear in her eyes that he'd seen yesterday when he'd told her to kiss him. Then he'd thought it was just the fear of confronting the attraction between them. Now he wasn't so sure. This was not flirtatious and teasing. This was something more. Something that instinctively he knew would demand so much more from him than just proving he desired her.

Rio could hardly believe it had come to this. Lysandros had unwittingly unleashed that painful moment when Hans had taken advantage of her. Now Lysandros demanded to know exactly what it was that had made her end things between them. But she couldn't tell him. If their engagement were real, if he truly wanted more than just passion from her, she might be able to. She could tell him if he felt the same way about her as she did about him, although she was fighting it with every breath. But none of this was real. Not the romantic breakfast. Not the ring on her finger. Not even wanting her to kiss him. It was all an act. An elaborate charade from a man who didn't want a deeper or emotional relationship.

'It was more the situation than you.' Rio bluffed her way out of the corner she'd managed to back herself into. She couldn't tell him anything now.

Hans had most definitely taken advantage of all her barriers being lowered. He might no longer be a threat to her, or any other woman, but Lysandros was. For very different reasons he was a threat to her. She *did* want more. Wanted him.

She longed to be held by him. Kissed by him. Longed for him to show her what passion and desire could truly be like. But she couldn't risk her heart. Not when she knew he'd already planned the end of their fake engagement.

'The situation?' His voice had deepened, impatience laced through it.

'I don't want to be engaged, Lysandros—to you or anyone else.'

'Neither do I.' The cold, hard truth rushed at her like an icy wave on the beach during an English winter. 'My ex-fiancée destroyed any ideals I had of marriage when she was unfaithful. Marriage is not for me.'

'But your mother is looking to you for grandchildren?' Curiosity forced the question out. Lysandros was finally allowing her to slip behind his defensive barrier.

'She is, but hopefully Xena will marry and one day have children—the next generation to inherit the family business.'

His emotionless words left her in no doubt how adamant he was about not being a father. It was another reason not to allow her emotions to become any more attached to him. She had begun to question her haste at ending their relationship, had started to see a different side to him. One that put her heart in danger, making her want a future with him, but now she knew it could never be.

'Lysandros…' she began cautiously, wishing she could tell him the truth, but the dark depths of his eyes, devoid of all emotion, snatched away her frail confidence, snuffed out the fleeting opportunity to say anything.

'I apologise for trying to kiss you just now.' The sincerity in his voice touched her heart, adding to her confusion of how she felt about him, what she really wanted. 'You have my word that I will not force you to do anything you do not want to do.'

He reached out and placed his hand over hers, sending a shock wave of pleasure rushing through her. It was a touch that told her he cared, told her he would be true to his word. 'If anything happens between us, it will be because *you* want it to.'

'What we had, before. It was good, but…' She paused as her heart and her head did battle. Her head won. The moment to tell him the truth had gone. 'I can never be what you need.'

'If that is what you believe then I must accept it.' The softness of his voice did untold things to her as her heart flipped over, disappointment filling her at what could have been, what could still be, if only she'd been brave enough. He made her feel unsure. She'd judged him harshly, believing his interest in her to be purely physical. Now she wasn't so convinced. Maybe beneath the hardened exterior he was far more tender and caring than he'd allowed her to think.

'And what about our so-called engagement? And the need to act out the romance?' She kept her voice brusque and businesslike, determined he wouldn't know just how much her heart was breaking right now.

'We need only return from this weekend as a happy couple. A bit of hand-holding and smiling should convince both Xena and my mother. I have business meetings all week, so you can have time alone with Xena on the island, but I would like you to attend the charity party in Athens next weekend.'

'Is that really necessary?' Her shoulders drooped at the thought of being paraded around publicly as his fiancée.

'Just a few hours at the party by my side, but the weekend away in Athens will further convince Xena and my mother that after I vowed I would never marry, you and I are engaged.'

'Do you honestly think that is necessary?'

He nodded. 'I do, Rio.' He looked at her, his eyes searching hers. 'We are doing this for Xena, remember?'

The unspoken words hung in the air between them. He was wrapping it all up as something honourable he was doing for his sister. And if she too wanted to help Xena, she had little choice but to accept his terms.

CHAPTER SIX

SINCE THEIR CONVERSATION on the beach Rio had been on edge. Completely trapped by this charade of an engagement. Lysandros hadn't spoken of it again during lunch on the yacht and had disappeared below deck soon afterwards, leaving her to enjoy the warm sunshine. She tried to put everything—the kiss, the engagement and him—out of her mind and relax, but just knowing he was nearby, just remembering the way he'd held her so gently, as if he cared, made that impossible.

'Would you like to have a swim?' Rio looked at Lysandros and her pulse leapt. He was wearing only black trunks. She couldn't take her eyes off him, the afternoon sunshine showcasing his toned physique to perfection. His bronzed skin glistened.

She blinked rapidly, fighting for words—any words. 'A swim?'

His wickedly sexy smile left her in no doubt he'd noticed her reaction to him as she'd studied the muscled contours of his tanned body. His roguish tone made her heart flip and her stomach flutter as he stood there expectantly, waiting for her to join him. All she could do was look up at him. All that exposed flesh. That overpoweringly sexy masculinity. Damn him. Was he doing it on purpose? Pushing her to the edge? Proving a point? That their attraction was far from over?

'Yes, a swim.' He reached for her hand, his arms flexing as his muscles rippled beneath the sun's rays. 'It's very freeing, swimming in the sea. You should try it.'

She thought of the costume she'd packed, the daring one Xena had convinced her to buy last year and she hadn't yet had the courage or opportunity to wear. It was the only one she had with her but the thought of swimming in the cool, clear waters was very tempting.

'I will go and change.' She allowed him to help her up, allowed him to keep her hand in his, her eyes firmly fixed on his face as she came up close to his muscled chest. She inhaled deeply, taking in his scent, making herself dizzy with desire. She'd never seen a man naked, or even been this close to one who was all but naked. He was totally over-powering.

'Don't be too long or I'll have to come and find you.' The teasing note of his voice sent a shiver of pleasure down her spine and she smiled boldly at him, feeling the Rio Hans had almost obliterated pushing back to the fore. She could feel herself beginning to relent, beginning to want Lysandros all over again. Her body wanted him, longed for what could have been. As did her heart. But her head continued to reign supreme, keeping her safe.

She laughed lightly, desperate to find herself again, to once more be the woman who had told Lysandros she wanted to be with him all night. 'In that case, I will be back as soon as I can.'

He raised his brows, a smile on his lips, disarming that all-too-powerful control he usually radiated but in turn ramping up his sex appeal. 'Make sure you are.'

She changed so quickly she didn't give herself time to worry about how the black swimsuit looked on her, how the cut-away waist made it virtually a bikini. She was too flustered by the image of Lysandros, burned into her mind, all but naked.

As she reached the bathing platform at the

end of the yacht she suddenly felt far too exposed. Lysandros was in the sea, his arms moving with ease as he trod water, his gaze all but devouring her. She could feel the heat of it from where she stood and the only way to avoid it was to either turn and run back to her cabin or jump into the water. His threat of coming to find her if she didn't join him filled her mind. It would be safer to be in the water than out of it.

Without any further hesitation she stepped off the bathing board and sank into the water. It was much cooler than she'd expected and she gasped with shock. She'd never swum in the sea before. At first there was a moment of panic as she sensed the depth below her, the vastness of the cool water around her. It reflected perfectly how she felt each time Lysandros looked at her, and those feelings were getting stronger. She panicked, unable to co-ordinate her arms and legs into anything that resembled swimming. The truth of her thoughts numbed her as rapidly as the cool water.

Just as she thought she was going under the surface of the water she felt Lysandros's arms around her, his body against hers as he pulled her close, powering them both the short distance back to the bathing board. Her breath was coming hard and fast as she looked up at him but it had nothing to do with the water. It had everything to do with the man who held her.

'Are you okay?' The same concern filled his voice that he'd shown her at the hospital when he'd crouched before her. She could almost believe he cared for her.

She should look away from him, try to avoid all he was fooling her into. She should move her body away from his, but she couldn't. A spell had been woven around them, wrapping them together in the water. 'I haven't done this before.'

Her breathless declaration left her wondering what she was referring to. Swimming in the sea or being held by a man who was almost naked, a man whose muscled body was pressed against hers as he held her. The cool water accentuated every move he made as he kept them afloat.

It was wild. Erotic. After her experience with Hans, it should make her panic, but that was the last thing she felt. Right now, she wanted to stay in Lysandros's arms, to savour the protection and safety offered by them. She looked into his eyes and knew it was too late.

She was falling for him all over again. She wanted him more than ever. If he tried to kiss her now she wouldn't ever want him to stop.

'I need a swim.' His voice was gruff as he let her go, leaving her clutching the bathing board rail. His eyes bored into hers and she couldn't find any words to hide how she felt right at this moment, to tell him she didn't want him to swim away from her.

With a rush of water, he pushed away from her, his strong arms taking him further away, further out of her reach. She should be glad because she'd been on the brink of kissing him, of allowing her body to beg for the kind of satisfaction she knew instinctively only he could give. But until she could tell him what had happened to her after the recital, there was too much between them still, even if the desire was burning higher than ever before.

She pulled herself out of the water, fighting the disappointment that he had kept his word. Annoyed with her warring emotions, she wrapped herself in a large towel, needing to calm the shivers that had more to do with Lysandros than the cool water. With a final glance back at his sexy body surging through the sea, she headed up onto the main deck. Even though she wanted to look back, to watch

him, she couldn't. Not when she was losing
her foolish and innocent heart to him all over
again.

Lysandros had stayed in the sea long after
Rio had gone back up on deck. He swam until
nearly all his strength had gone, knowing he
couldn't fight his desire for her much longer.
Whatever it was between them, it was far more
powerful than anything he'd ever known, and
as she'd almost gone beneath the surface of the
water, the overwhelming need to protect her,
keep her safe from everyone and everything,
had almost crushed him.

So much so that when he'd held that sexy
body close to his all he'd wanted was to make
her completely his, to show her that passion
wasn't something to be afraid of, that desire—
their desire—was something to be cherished.

But he'd let her go. He hadn't trusted himself. Not after the promise he'd made to her
that nothing would happen she didn't want to
happen. The only person who could set light
to the passion that simmered between them
was Rio. He'd given her his word and never
went back on it.

When he joined Rio on deck he'd regained
his control and that sexy black one-piece was

thankfully well covered with a long black dress. Even so, the image of her as she'd stood at the stern of his yacht was there each time he blinked, as if he'd just looked into the brightest of lights.

Music, he decided, would take his mind off the erotic thoughts of Rio that crowded in on him, and he pressed the remote on the sound system. He stood with his back to Rio as the notes of the piano began to drift on the sea breeze. It would calm him and he fully expected it to please Rio as it was after all her instrument, but when he turned she looked more agitated than he'd ever seen her.

'This is one of Xena's favourites,' she said, her brow creased in worry, and all the desire he'd been fighting since he'd held her in the water threatened to take over. But he couldn't allow it, couldn't be the one to start things. It had to be Rio's choice, especially when the cloud of fear he'd seen on her face the day he'd arrived at the hospital still lingered around her.

'You should play for Xena when we return to the villa.' It was only now he realised he hadn't heard her play since she'd arrived.

'I'm not about to sit down and play for Xena when she has no hope of playing the violin for a long time.' The anger in her words raised his suspicion levels.

'Her wrist will heal, but it is more important to help her recover her memory. Listening to you play might do that.'

Rio paced away from him, the black dress moulding itself against her long limbs in the late afternoon wind, but their discussion meant he had to ignore that. She turned to look at him and he knew there was far more she was keeping from him.

'What is it, Rio? What are you worried about? Scared of even?' He watched her as she paced away from him, agitation in every step. Her whole body was tense and he knew for sure she was keeping something from him. Something big.

'You can tell me, Rio. Whatever it is.'

She turned to look at him, her face pale. 'That's just it. I can't.' Her voice had risen in exasperation and every nerve in his body was alert to the danger of being drawn into her emotions. But he'd been right. There *was* something she was keeping back.

Behind her the sun was sinking lower, creating a fusion of oranges across the sky, but all he could think about was his inability to deal with emotions. He didn't know what to do, what to say. Not when he'd spent his entire adult life hiding from all emotions but those that drove him in business, made him successful. Even as a child he'd remained behind a barrier so high that only the most determined family members had reached him.

His father had never been one of them. His father had been equally as unreachable.

As an adult Lysandros had decided his father must have been as emotionless as him, the pair of them so similar they'd retreated even further from one another. As a child, the only kind of sensible excuse for his father's aloofness he'd come up with had been that he'd never wanted to be a father.

That theory had been blown away after Xena had arrived. A baby his parents hadn't planned or expected, but one his father seemed able to shower with love and affection. The exact opposite of what he had received from his father.

Convinced he was somehow at fault, he'd buried his emotions. Now Rio's obvious distress was slowly chipping away at his armour.

'Why can't you, Rio?' He wanted to go to her, take her hands in his and reassure her. He wanted to look into her eyes while stroking his thumb over the back of her hand, wanted to offer the kind of comfort she wouldn't be threatened by, but his long-held instinct to stand in the shadows of emotion prevented him from moving.

'I just can't.'

'Is it to do with Xena? The accident?'

She looked at him, wide-eyed with shock. She held his gaze as she hugged her arms around herself, giving herself the kind of re-assurance, the comfort he should be giving her right now.

Again, there was that hesitation he was quickly realising Rio hid behind when forced to admit difficult things.

'As I told you, Xena and I had had a falling-out that night.' Her eyelashes covered her eyes, shielding her emotions from him as she looked down. He should be furious, should demand why, force her to tell the truth, but he couldn't summon any of those feelings. Strange new feelings were filling him and he crossed the deck and went to her.

Slowly he lifted her chin with his thumb and finger, wanting her to look into his eyes. When she did it was like being struck in the solar plexus. Never had he experienced such a strong urge to protect, to comfort.

'Why?' he asked gently, coaxing her, needing to know why she was so upset, so fearful.

'I should have supported her, but we'd been arguing and it seemed best to leave her to sleep. If only I'd known she would go out later, after I had gone to bed myself.' She tried to look down, but he kept her looking into his eyes.

'What were you arguing about?' Everything she was saying showed how jumbled her emotions were, and even though it would be pushing her when she was so very vulnerable, he needed to know this, sure it was crucial to Xena's memory loss.

'We'd fallen out over the man Xena was seeing.'

'Xena was in a relationship?' This was news to him.

'Yes, but it's over between them now,' Rio said almost in a whisper as she looked at him, panic in her eyes. 'Please don't let on to Xena that you know.'

A swift and uncomfortable knowledge that his own sister hadn't wanted him to know about her romance, that she hadn't felt able to confide in him, all but knocked the breath from his body.

'And has Xena remembered this man?'

Rio shook her head, the movement forcing him to let her go. 'He is just another of the bad events she seems to have blocked out.'

'Another bad event?' There were other things Xena couldn't remember besides the accident? Besides this man? Things that Rio clearly could.

Rio realised her mistake and moved away from him, away from his scrutiny. He needed to know what those bad things were but didn't know what to ask first. Should he demand to know the name of the man Xena was seeing? Or should he ask what other things his sister was blocking out?

The soft strains of the piano filled the warm evening air, the romantic notes in complete contrast to the wild emotions Rio had unleashed in him. The angry kind of emotions he was far more accustomed to dealing with.

'His name is Ricardo,' Rio began as she went and sat on the large luxury sofa, offering a view of the stunning sunset. 'He and Xena had been dating for several months.'

'Why didn't Xena want me to know?' He asked the question that had been racing round his mind. What had his sister been hiding?

* * *

Rio didn't know what to say. Tell him the truth and betray Xena's confidence or push Lysandros further away from her when she was finally beginning to rediscover the romance that had been between them before Hans had destroyed it?

Lysandros looked at her and for the first time she saw this powerful businessman, who was used to having everything exactly as he wanted, was struggling to understand what he'd learnt. He looked as vulnerable as she felt.

'Why, Rio?' His tone was soft but full of desperation. He really did love Xena. Even if he kept it well hidden from everyone—including himself. He loved his sister. Rio's heart wrenched and the need to go to him, to hold him, to let him know it was okay to be vulnerable, okay to feel love, rushed through her.

'You must never tell Xena I have told you,' she said with a firmness that surprised both her and him. 'I would never normally betray a friend's confidence like this, but Xena's amnesia isn't a normal circumstance.'

He frowned, his eyes full of questions. 'What is it, Rio?'

'Ricardo was married,' she said softly, allowing the implications to settle between them, to infiltrate the cracking barriers around him.

He turned from her and she dragged in a sharp breath. She hadn't expected that. Rage maybe, definitely anger, but not this. Xena had filled her in on his first engagement, on the fiancée who had had an affair and left him just days before the wedding ceremony. It was little wonder he was so against infidelity.

She crossed the distance to him, her attention fixed on his broad, tense shoulders. 'Xena told me why you would be angry she was seeing a married man. She said it was because of your father, the way he broke up the family when Xena was very young.'

He glanced down at her, the expression in his eyes unreadable. 'But she got involved with him? Continued the affair?'

Rio placed her hand on his arm, feeling the heat of his tanned skin beneath her fingers. 'She never wanted to hurt you. That's why she didn't tell you.'

For a moment his eyes searched hers, all barriers down, all the emotion he kept locked away showing in them.

'You must have loved your fiancée very much,' Rio said, hardly able to voice it. *She* was now his fiancée. His temporary fiancée. But he would never love her like that.

'My fiancée?' The barriers slammed back down. Firmness filled his voice.

'Yes. Xena said…' Rio stumbled over her words, caught off guard by the sudden change in him. 'She said you were engaged once.'

'I was, yes.' Now he sounded as if he was talking to a stranger. About a stranger. Every trace of gentleness had gone. 'She didn't want to get married—at least, not to me. Instead of being honest, telling me, she left with her new lover.'

'I'm sorry,' she whispered.

'It was one big web of deceit.' He looked at her, that dark coldness filling his eyes again.

'But we aren't being truthful to anyone now.' She grasped at her reasons for not wanting to accept his fake engagement deal—all the people who were going to be upset when he ended the engagement. Xena. His mother. Thank goodness she hadn't told her parents anything yet. They had always harboured hopes she'd meet the right man and would get married.

'Maybe we are,' he said softly as he turned to her, taking her hand from his arm, holding it in his. The expression in his eyes had changed.

The coldness had gone, the building intensity of desire replacing it.

If only she could trust his desire, that softening of his demeanour. She blinked back the tears threatening to spill in the emotion of the moment, because when he looked at her like that she could forget everything.

'There is one truth, though, Rio.' His voice softened, the seductive sound making her heart flutter, raising her hopes, making her fall for him that little bit more.

'There is?' Was that husky whisper really hers?

His thumb caressed her hand, the sensation making her want so much more. She wanted him to hold all of her, not just her hand.

'I'm very attracted to you, Rio. That is very much true.'

She looked up at him, his declaration only confirming that for him what was between them was simply physical. She might have once started to hope it could be different, but those words warned that wasn't possible. And if it was, would he really want her after she'd given him such a clear message of wanting to sleep with him and then standing him up? He had no idea she was a virgin, no idea just how big a step that was for her. If they did continue their romance—for real, not because of a fake engagement—would he expect to go back to that moment? Expect her to sleep with him straight away?

She might be regaining the confidence to admit she was attracted to him, that she did want to have the night she'd almost had in his bed, but she wasn't ready to put her heart on the line yet. Before she could even think of being intimate with him, she had to tell him. Had to risk him turning his back on her for good.

'I know I said I wouldn't do anything you didn't want to do, but...' He paused, gently brushing her hair back from her face, and she couldn't take her eyes from him. 'I want to kiss you, Rio.'

Heaven help her, if she didn't move away, *she* would kiss *him*.

She could feel herself leaning towards him, feel the heat of need firing up within her. His gaze was fixed to hers, his eyes darkening rapidly, intensely. 'Lysandros...' she whispered huskily.

He took that as an invitation, brushing his lips teasingly and tantalisingly over hers. She closed her eyes as her need rose to new heights, and kissed him gently. He didn't reach for her, didn't take her in his arms, and for that she was thankful. Whether he intended it or not, he'd left her in complete control and she took it, opening her eyes and stepping back away from the temptation of all his kiss had offered—all she wanted.

CHAPTER SEVEN

THE IMAGE OF RIO, looking up at him as they'd stood so close together on his yacht, passion and doubt filling her eyes, had haunted Lysandros all week. The feel of her lips still burned on his as she'd lightly kissed him, almost relenting, almost giving in to desire. Then she'd stepped back from him, forcing him to honour the promise he'd given her. Her doubt, her pure vulnerability, had made him cut short their weekend and return her to the safety of Xena's company on the island late that evening.

He'd left for Athens immediately afterwards, needing to put as much distance as possible between him and the temptation she represented, hoping that a week of meetings and deals would smother the emotions, the need that just looking into her eyes created within him.

As soon as Rio had arrived at his penthouse apartment this morning, he'd known that hope had been futile. The desire between them now so high it was like tinder-dry grass being scorched in the summer sun. One tiny spark and it would ignite, but after his promise, the only one of them who could produce that spark was Rio.

He took a deep and steadying breath and waited for her to emerge from her room. Since she'd arrived, the apartment had become a flurry of activity as deliveries of everything from dresses to shoes and bags had arrived for her. She and Xena had obviously been busy after he'd left the island and, needing space and time to strengthen his resolve not to touch Rio, he'd left for the office. This evening, when she accompanied him to the charity ball, was going to test that resolve to the absolute maximum.

The door to her room clicked and opened and he turned to her as she emerged, but nothing could have prepared him for the elegant vision that stood on the threshold of her room, regarding him apprehensively—or the way his body reacted as lust throbbed urgently through him.

'You look stunning,' he said, walking towards her. The dark blue silk dress complemented her complexion perfectly and the plunging neckline did little to calm the desire he was already struggling to control for this woman. He wanted her with a passion he'd never known before. A passion that threatened to consume him totally.

All he could think of was how her body had moulded to his as he'd held her in the sea. The look on her face, her hair wet and slicked back, her eyelashes holding droplets of water, had created such a sexy image it would be branded for ever in his memory. Now this new sophisticated and daringly sexy version of Rio would join that memory.

'Xena assured me it was perfect for this evening's party.' She looked down at herself, picking up the soft silk of the skirt, pulling out the folds of the fabric, before dropping them and trying to adjust the daringly low neckline. So he was right about Xena's influence on all the purchases. She looked back at him nervously, the sexy and confident woman of moments ago slipping away. In her place was a woman very vulnerable, very innocent.

'Beautiful.' He wasn't referring to the dress but the woman wearing it.

'It is beautiful, but I haven't ever worn anything so daring. Xena is so much more adventurous than I am and you know how she is once she gets an idea into her head.'

He moved closer to Rio, unable to stop himself. He'd punished himself all week by throwing himself into his work and he hadn't realised how much he'd missed her company. 'You look amazing, Rio. Every man there tonight will be looking at you.'

'That's exactly what I don't want.' She almost gasped the words out. 'I don't want that kind of attention.'

He frowned, thinking of the gowns he'd seen her wearing before. Something wasn't making sense. 'The dress is beautiful, as are you.'

The level of protectiveness he felt for Rio was far beyond anything he'd known before. All he wanted was to look after her, care for her and keep her safe. It wasn't just because she was his sister's friend. It was deeper than that. It was also something he wasn't remotely ready to acknowledge, let alone explore.

'I just feel…' She searched for the right word. '…vulnerable.'

'Relax,' he said softly, and stepped close enough to inhale the light floral scent of her perfume. Instinctively he reached out and brushed back a stray strand of hair that had already broken free from her elaborately pinned-up hair. 'I will be at your side all night—if you want me to be.'

'I do,' she whispered, sending his pulse rate rocketing, and the heavy throb of desire struck up a constant drumming round his body. Were they finally getting back to that moment at the recital? The moment when she'd told him she wanted to be his all night?

'In that case, it will be an honour to have a beautiful woman on my arm.' He'd have to be blind not to have noticed the soft swell of her breasts, and he wondered if Xena was aware just how self-conscious Rio had become. He hadn't seen Rio like this before and Xena wouldn't be so insensitive as to insist such a dress be sent here for her if she was aware Rio felt like this. But then Xena still hadn't recovered her memory, and maybe, if things were normal, she would have known how uncomfortable Rio would be with a dress like that. 'All I can say is that Xena made the right choice.'

She blushed and looked down, but didn't step away. 'Thank you.' She paused and looked back up at him. 'For looking after me, for being patient.' She blinked as if considering whether to add something to that, finally succumbing to the temptation. 'And for not pushing me into anything, despite what I said at the recital.'

He took her hand in his and, looking into the depths of her eyes, he saw her pupils expand, saw the unveiled attraction shining in them. That pulse of desire leapt within him. She might be holding back on him, but she wanted him with the same kind of intensity with which he wanted her. Whatever her reason for calling things off, it couldn't be a lack of attraction or desire.

'We are in a strange situation,' he said softly as he stroked his thumb over her hand, the best way he could convey his respect for her. 'Our engagement is not real, and as you know all about my first encounter with engagement, I hope you can understand why it can't be.'

Lysandros imagined being engaged to Rio for real. Imagined planning to make her his wife, the woman he would spend the rest of his life with, and was shocked that the idea was far from unappealing.

'I do,' she said softly, so softly it sounded filled with regret.

'But there is one thing that is very real. The desire between us. I feel it every time I am near you. It tests my promise to you every time I look in your eyes and see desire in them.'

She took in a deep and ragged breath but didn't pull her hand back from his. 'It tests me too, Lysandros,' she said in a shaky whisper.

He lifted her hand to his lips, brushing a lingering kiss over her soft skin. That touch stirred all the longing he'd had for her since the first day Xena had introduced them. From their very first date he'd promised himself he would take things slowly, go at the pace Rio was comfortable with. He just hadn't expected her to shut him out of her life, not when they had been getting on so well and especially not when the sexual tension between them had increased with each date.

'There is something I should tell you, Lysandros.' Rio's voice wavered with emotion, or was it fear? 'Something that may douse that desire entirely.'

'Then tell me, Rio. Whatever it is, tell me. It's driving me mad.'

'I want to, but not now. There isn't time. We need to go to the charity ball.' Nerves hovered in those statements, showing him so much more than she knew, and he accepted that now was not the time to press her for more details.

'You can tell me, Rio,' he reassured her. 'Whenever you are ready, you can tell me.'

'Thank you.' She lowered her lashes, looking up at him shyly and smiling. 'I will. Soon. When I'm ready.'

He knew he'd have to accept that. Whatever it was between them, preventing the desire from flowing freely, would be removed, but not until she was ready.

'My car is waiting,' he said brusquely, pushing down his need for her. 'We should go now.'

Before I forget my patience and kiss you. Prove to you that nothing else matters.

Lysandros had been true to his word all evening and Rio had enjoyed the charity ball, where she was more than a little shocked to discover he was the patron for the charity. She stood now at the front of the gathered crowd, listening to the applause for the speech he'd just given. It might have been in Greek but she knew from the nodding heads of approval and the applause that he'd made an impact on those here tonight, that they respected him. It was clear that the charity to help families in crisis in Greece was one he was passionate about.

From the stage he looked down at her, smiling at her, before speaking again in Greek. As the applause slowed, her heart lurched, forcing her to suck in a deep breath. His tall, athletic physique, which she'd seen on the yacht and had tried desperately to ignore, couldn't be disguised completely by his black tuxedo.

He looked devastatingly handsome, the kind of man who would break a girl's heart, but he'd been so sweet, so gentle and patient since she'd arrived in Athens. It made her admit she'd missed him last week once he'd left the island. During the weekend on his yacht she'd almost forgotten her fears of being physical with him, almost forgotten why she'd ended things between them. Now, after his subtly seductive gestures, entwined with such caring patience, before they'd left the apartment, she couldn't help but want more. She wanted him to kiss her, to hold her and caress away that last lingering fear.

And she wanted that, wanted him—tonight. But first she had to tell him. Their engagement might not be real, but the raw sexual desire between them was. Despite always envisaging giving her virginity to the man she loved, the man she would one day marry, she couldn't walk away from Lysandros now and not know the joy of being completely his. Even if it was for one night only. Especially now she was sure it was what she needed to lock away the past for ever.

The lights dimmed, snagging her from her thoughts, and a round of applause broke out again, confusing Rio. Or was it the handsome Greek walking towards her, intent and purpose in his eyes as those around her moved back, allowing him through the crowd until he stood before her and took her hands in his?

'I ended my speech by saying I would open the dancing with my fiancée.' He smiled at her, mischief in his eyes, laughter in his voice, and her stomach somersaulted. 'Will you do me the honour? Or are you going to make me look a complete fool?'

She laughed at him, feeling more at ease in his company than she'd ever felt with any man. 'Just to save you from ridicule, I will dance with you.'

He took her hand and led her to the dance floor as the applause continued. When he took her in his arms she didn't feel awkward, as she'd expected to do. It felt so right to feel the heat of his body, his strength as he held her close. Right and exciting. It made that realisation of moments ago even stronger.

'I think I have shocked just about every person here.' He spoke softly as he lowered his head close to hers, so close that if she turned just a fraction she would be able to tilt her chin up and kiss him.

Heat coursed through her. Not because of her thoughts but because of how much she wanted it to happen. She wanted to feel his lips on hers once more. Really feel them. She wanted to taste the exquisite pleasure of being desired by Lysandros.

'Because you are dancing?' she teased with a coy smile, trying not to give in to the need surging through her so wildly.

'Maybe, but I think it has more to do with the fact that I am engaged to the most beautiful woman in the room.' His sexy, desire-laden voice sent a tremor of pure pleasure hurtling around her.

'Then maybe I should shock them too.' Her rediscovered desire for Lysandros gave her the kind of boldness she'd only just begun to explore the afternoon of the recital. That boldness now made her daring—flirty.

His brows rose suggestively as they moved slowly around the dance floor, other couples now joining them. 'And how would you do that?'

Rio lowered her lashes, suddenly shy, but when she raised them again and looked into the inky blackness of his eyes, swirling with desire, she knew fighting it was pointless. From the very first day they'd met something had sparked to life between them, something powerful and undeniable. She couldn't deny that she wanted this man to kiss her, to touch her and to love her.

Almost all the barriers she'd put up around herself, around her heart, long before Hans's attack, crashed down as she reached up to press her lips to his. The warmth of his lips melted to hers and she closed her eyes, savouring the heady sensation, wanting to lose herself in its pleasure for ever.

His hand brushed over her cheek, into her hair, pulling down some of the elaborate hairstyle she'd had painstakingly done only hours ago. It felt like they were swaying as the pleasure of his kiss took over. Why had she resisted him for so long? Why hadn't she been brave enough to admit she wanted him?

Because then you weren't ready.

Now she was.

The words swirled around in her mind as he slowly pulled away from her. 'That was magnificent acting,' he said in a hoarse whisper. 'Nobody will ever question our engagement now.'

'It wasn't acting.' She forced herself to continue looking at him, even though she wanted to look down, lessen the intensity of the emotions that shrouded them in a mist of desire.

His sexy, lingering smile made her surer than ever that she was finally ready to leave the past behind, finally ready to explore the joy of being loved by a man. She trusted Lysandros. He'd let his guard down, revealed the kind of man he truly was—a man burned by love, unable to trust the emotion again. That vulnerability helped her, as did his patience. Despite the tough devil-may-care attitude he showed to the world, the hard-edged businessman he portrayed himself as, he was a gentle, compassionate man. Hope began to grow within her. Hope that something more could come of their fake engagement, rekindling all she'd begun to feel about him when they'd been dating. Her emotions freed themselves from behind the defensive wall she'd retreated to after the attack.

'It's a good job we are surrounded by so many people at this moment.' His accent had deepened, his voice almost cracking with desire, heightening her need for him, her need to be kissed by him—and so much more.

'Why?' she teased, the power of being desired dizzying, as if she'd drunk far too much champagne.

'Why?' He tightened his hold on her, his hand at her back searing through the fabric of her gown. 'Because I would not be able to stop at kissing you.'

'I don't want you to.' She closed her eyes as a shudder of desire rushed through her. She swallowed, hardly able to believe what was happening, what she was about to admit, that she was finally ready to move on from that terrifying moment with Hans. 'I want you to kiss me.'

'Rio.' He whispered her name, the raw desire in his voice almost too much. 'Are you sure this is what you want?'

She could feel him breathing deeply against her, each breath pressing against her breasts, and she knew she would never be surer of anything in her life. She wanted Lysandros, wanted him to make love to her, but not until she'd walked out from beneath the shadow of what Hans had done. Not until Lysandros knew why she'd stood him up. 'It is, but…'

He brushed his lips over hers then spoke softly, his lips so close it was wildly erotic to feel his breath on her lips. 'I promised you nothing would happen until you want it to and I meant it.'

She looked into his eyes, saw the smouldering desire but knew he really did mean it. She was totally in control and that was exactly what she needed to know.

The hum of desire still ruled her body as Rio walked into Lysandros's apartment. The short time in the chauffeur-driven car hadn't lessened any of that sexual tension, hadn't made her change her mind, but nerves were beginning to rush over her. Before anything could happen, she had to tell him why she'd stood him up that night after the recital.

Nerves fluttered inside her. It was more than just what Hans had done. She was a virgin. She was choosing, this moment, to give him something very precious. Should she say something? Would he know if she didn't? Would he be able to tell that the emotions she was experiencing were so very new to her?

'Champagne?' His question arced through the air, pulsating through the heady desire that still had them in its grip. Nerves added to the powerful cocktail of feelings and made her skin tingle as if tiny flakes of snow were falling on her.

'Champagne sounds perfect,' she said, glad of the time to compose herself, to prepare to tell him what he deserved to know. Instinctively she walked over to the grand piano standing proudly by the windows that gave an unrivalled view of Athens. She wanted to reach out and touch it, to touch the keys, but not yet. 'There is something I need to tell you.'

She had his full attention now as he stood, the unopened bottle in his hand. 'What is it, Rio?' The gentleness of his voice gave her the strength she needed to finally tell him why she'd called off their blossoming romance.

'The reason I didn't meet you for dinner that night...' She paused, trying to gauge his reaction, but his eyes were full of concern and she knew she had to say it. 'It was because I was scared.'

'You were scared?' The incredulity in his voice was too much and she drew in a deep, ragged breath.

'Not of you, but of what I'd told you I wanted.'

'That you wanted to be with me all night?'

She nodded, her eyes locking with his across the apartment. He hadn't moved but the intensity in his eyes, the desire he couldn't hide, gave her the courage to continue. 'That was what I wanted that night—and it's what I want tonight.'

He put the bottle down and walked over to her, a frown on his face, his breathing fast and shallow. 'I want that, Rio, so much,' he said as he took her hands in his, and the sincerity in his voice almost broke her heart, it sounded so full of love. Or was that just her foolish heart believing what it really wanted to see, to hear, to feel? 'But I don't want you to be scared. I meant what I said about not doing anything you didn't want to do. You are in full control.'

'I'm grateful for that, thank you,' she whispered. 'But there is something else I need to tell you first.'

He brushed her hair back from her face so tenderly she almost closed her eyes, expecting him to kiss her. But he didn't. 'Tell me,' he whispered so softly it was almost impossible to hear him.

'After the recital I went to one of the practice rooms. Hans had arranged to meet me there, to go over some of my final pieces of the season. I was playing when he came in, so I didn't hear him. He'd been drinking and…' Her words stumbled to a halt and she swallowed hard as Lysandros appeared to hold his breath. She didn't know if she could finish, didn't know if she could admit it aloud. After she'd given her statement the only other person she'd told had been Xena. She'd understood why she couldn't see Lysandros any more, had supported her through it, but the accident had claimed those memories, along with the other bad events of recent weeks.

'What happened, Rio?' His voice was so gentle that it didn't fit with the hard lines of his jaw as he clenched it and looked down at her.

'He...he...' She looked up at him anxiously, not wanting to say it but knowing she had to, for herself as well as Lysandros. 'He thought I was interested in him, that I was playing just for him, and he tried to...'

Fury blazed in Lysandros's eyes, but he remained calm and still, giving her the strength to finish telling him. 'Only tried?'

'He took advantage of the fact that I was sitting at the piano and grabbed me. I managed to push him away and should have run, but I was too shocked. Then he tried to kiss me, tried to...' She shuddered at the memory of Hans pawing at her and the way her heart had raced as she'd lashed out at him, shocked by the intensity of it.

A harsh expletive tore from Lysandros and she blinked. 'Did he hurt you?' he growled.

She began to wonder if she'd done the right thing. Had she ruined the moment between them? 'No, thanks to Judith and two other men.' She closed her eyes against the memory, willing herself not to get upset all over again. Hans wasn't worth another tear. 'I went home with Judith after I'd given the police my statement. I just couldn't face you or Xena.'

'I understand, Rio.' He looked at her, full of compassion as he brushed his hand over her hair soothingly. 'Of course you didn't want to see me after that. Does Xena know?'

'Yes, but she seems to have blocked it out too,' she said, and finally looked down, away from his gaze. She'd just ruined the one chance she might have had at discovering intimacy with the man she loved.

'Can I hold you?' She looked up again. He still wanted her, but more than that, he was thinking of her just by asking.

'Yes,' she whispered, hope that he could one day love her blotting out the bitterness of all she'd just told him. 'Please, hold me.'

His arms wrapped around her, holding her to him. His gentleness was so unexpected after the firmness of his expression as she'd told him that her breath rushed from her in a gasp.

She nestled herself against him, feeling safe and secure.

'Thank you for telling me,' he said as his lips pressed into her hair, but unlike the time on the beach she didn't pull away. It was a caring and loving gesture and exactly what she wanted.

'It scared me so much I just couldn't see you. I'm so sorry for standing you up.' Her voice was muffled by his tuxedo and she breathed in his scent, gathering strength from it.

'I understand, Rio, and it's okay. It wasn't your fault.' His voice was gentle as he lifted her chin with his thumb, and she looked up at him, seeing the sincerity in his eyes. 'We don't have to do anything you don't want to.'

'I know,' she whispered as desire began to sluice away the fear of a night that had almost lost her Lysandros. She wasn't going to allow Hans to dictate her future, her emotions any more. 'But I meant what I said. I want to be with you tonight.'

'Are you sure?' His eyes searched hers.

She smiled and stretched up to place her lips against his in a lingering and tender kiss. She didn't want to talk about the past any more, didn't want it to spoil things. She wanted to bring everything back to where they'd been as he'd been about to open the champagne, only now without that devastating secret between them.

'I am.' She smiled, pleased to see desire in his eyes once more. 'Did you say something about champagne?'

She watched intently as he popped the cork on the champagne, nerves and excitement whirling around inside her. She returned to the piano, reaching out her fingers, tracing them lightly over the keys, the past now banished by his understanding. She wanted him to make love to her, wanted him to be her first lover, and she would take this moment for what it was. Even though her heart was fast becoming his, she knew he was not the kind of man to give his. Not that it mattered now. She was beginning to fall in love with him and becoming truly his was all she wanted tonight.

Tomorrow didn't matter—just tonight.

Without thinking about what she was doing, she pulled out the piano stool and seated herself before the black and white keys that had tormented her for so many weeks since the attack. She could hear the fizz of the champagne as Lysandros poured two glasses and knew that placing her fingers on the keys and playing was as much a part of this healing process as giving herself willingly to the man who was, at least for now, her fiancé. She wanted to be loved by him, to experience a night of passion with him, but first she *had* to do this.

It was another way of putting aside that terrible afternoon.

He placed the glasses of champagne on the piano and stood at its side, questions in his eyes. She kept her focus on the piano keys in front of her, grateful he hadn't voiced those questions, hadn't broken the spell that was propelling her to do this—towards him.

She took a deep breath, lifted her hands onto the keys once more, poised and ready to play.

Lysandros remained silent but moved to stand behind her, out of her line of vision. After what Hans had done, it should have made her nervous, but she trusted Lysandros. Not seeing him but knowing he was there, that he was with her on this healing journey, enabled her to focus. She loved him even more for his patience, his understanding. As if he knew this was something she had to do before they could become lovers.

Her index finger pressed one note. She stopped. Was she ready for this? She didn't know, but whatever this was, it was far more than just playing the piano again. She sat, locked in her own world of turmoil.

Lysandros remained behind her. She was acutely aware of him standing there, of his presence, his patience, giving her strength. She took another breath, closed her eyes, slipping into that magical zone she always went to when she played. For the first time since the attempt by Hans to take from her what she hadn't wanted to give, she was ready to allow all her emotions to flow from her and onto the keys. She pulled back her hands.

She could do this. She could play the piano again *and* be with the man she loved.

CHAPTER EIGHT

LYSANDROS HELD HIS breath as he waited for Rio to play the first notes. The tension in the air was heavy. He'd seen her hesitation, knew it was because of all she'd told him and the worry of his reaction. He was as mad as hell, but he'd remained calm. For Rio's sake, he'd kept all his anger in, understanding now why she'd stood him up and then ended things.

If he was more able to connect emotionally with people, Rio may have confided in him, instead of ending things. But she hadn't because of his damned male pride, along with his inability to allow emotions in. But Rio was changing all that, smashing down barrier after barrier, allowing emotions to escape and be felt, not just him but her too.

He looked at Rio as she sat at the piano stool, his heart constricting so hard it hurt. He heard her draw in a deep breath and held his as she lifted her hands to the keys before pulling them back in hesitation. She needed to play right now, needed to let out everything she'd been holding back, everything about Hans, about him, about Xena's accident. He knew instinctively she needed that before anything could happen between them.

He also knew better than to break a musician's concentration and focus, yet he wanted her to know he understood. Not just that she needed to play now, but why. He moved back towards her, stood behind her, about to rest his hands on her shoulders when he remembered how she'd described Hans behind her. He moved away, relieved he hadn't destroyed the moment as she began to play.

The first notes were tentative, unsure. Then more notes followed until he recognised the first movement of Beethoven's *Moonlight Sonata*. The sound of the piano filled his apartment. The soft, slow notes, so full of emotion it was as if he was at his own private concert, as if she was playing just for him—for them.

He clenched his jaw, balling his hands into tight fists as need for Rio rocketed beyond anything he'd ever known. Each note smashed at the barriers around his emotions, the tension in the air increasing to almost suffocating levels. All he could think about was making love to her. He wanted Rio with a need reaching fever pitch, and as the notes were played with more conviction, he became convinced she was letting him know, through each seductive bar of music, that she wanted him too. That nothing else other than the two of them mattered. That tonight belonged to them alone.

He moved slowly away from the temptation Rio created, trying to focus on the lights of Athens, but it was too much. He had to see her, had to watch her, and turned his attention back to Rio at the piano. Her body swayed in gentle motion with the music, her fingers caressing and stroking the keys, making him wish it was his body she was touching so lovingly. The low-cut back of her dress was showing off her spine, each movement she made more erotic than the last. The ferocity with which he wanted her took his breath away, but he was careful not to scare her, not after what she'd just told him. He wanted this moment, tonight, to be special for her.

Several strands of her hair had fallen down and he longed to push them aside and kiss the pale skin of her neck. He wanted to inhale her scent, to taste her skin. How could a piece of music become so erotic?

Because the woman you want is playing it.

Rio stroked her long, slender fingers down the keys, her engagement ring catching the light and sparkling as she played the final notes of the first movement. Then, still locked in her emotional cocoon, she slowly laid her palms on her lap, her concert training still ruling despite the heightened sexual tension sparking around them.

The notes of the piano faded away and silence hung heavy as he stood, waiting for her to come back from whatever place it was musicians went to when they'd invested every ounce of emotion into their performance. His breathing deepened, became heavy, as if he had been kissing her for the last five minutes instead of listening to her play.

'There is only one thing more beautiful than hearing you play and that is watching you play.' His voice was husky with desire, and drinking the remainder of his champagne in one go, he tried to hold himself back, something he was not at all used to doing.

Rio turned to face him. 'I've never played to a man like that before.' She blushed and looked beyond him, out of the window, seemingly losing herself in the night view of the city he now called home.

'Then I am honoured.' He picked up her glass of champagne, not wanting her to think about the practice session she'd had with that vile man. He didn't want her to ever have to think about that again. With a smile he handed the glass to her, his fingers inadvertently brushing against hers. Had she crossed some sort of barrier by playing like that to him? 'Was that the first time you have played since…?' He didn't want to say the word 'attack'; he didn't want to bring it all back to her.

She looked up at him, searching his eyes, and he didn't miss the hesitation. 'Yes,' she whispered, so softly, so seductively he wanted to lean down and kiss her, but if he did, he wouldn't be able to stop. He'd want more, much more. 'I couldn't even sit at the piano. Then Xena had the accident.'

She stood up, bringing herself so close to him that he'd swear she knew exactly what she was doing, just how teasing it was to have her delicious body, only partially concealed by the dark blue silk of her gown, so very close to him.

'Xena will be okay,' he said softly as he reached out and stroked her cheek. 'I want you to be okay too.'

'Me?' Those long lashes fluttered down again, closing her off to him.

'Yes, Rio, you.' He lifted her chin with his finger until she looked up at him. 'I want you to be happy, I want to make things right for you, but I'm fighting really hard here because I want to kiss you so much.' All he wanted was to lose himself in the pleasure Rio's body promised and give her that same pleasure.

Rio didn't want to feel the pain crashing forward when he mentioned Xena. Neither did she want to remember the fear of the afternoon Hans had tried to kiss her, tried to touch her. She didn't want anything other than to abandon herself to the intensity of the desire that filled the air like the heat before a thunderstorm.

'I want you to kiss me,' she whispered. The sound was so tremulous she wondered if he'd heard her.

The fire of desire erupted in his eyes and doubts assailed her but she forced them back. She didn't want to hear them, didn't want to allow them to take away this moment. She wanted Lysandros, wanted him to kiss her and so much more.

His eyes grew darker than the night sky

hanging above the ancient city beyond the windows. She couldn't look away, the fizz of desire arcing between them so powerfully. He didn't say anything, didn't acknowledge her words. Instead he moved closer, holding her face lightly in his hands as his lips gently met hers. A sigh of pleasure escaped from her and in her mind the happier notes of the *Moonlight Sonata*'s second movement played. This was right. So very right. She allowed the pleasure of his kiss to wrap around her.

She tasted champagne as his tongue slicked along her lips, then slid between them to entwine with hers. The stab of desire deep within her was so strong all she could do was answer his unspoken demands and deepen the kiss. The world swayed and she wanted to reach out to him, to put her arms around his neck and press herself against his body. It felt wanton and wild but so very right.

He let go of her abruptly, stepping back from her, the dim light of the apartment casting his face in shadow, making it impossible to read his emotions, his thoughts. All she could do was stand still, breathing deep and hard, her body pulsing with a hungry need that only he could satisfy.

'Don't stop, Lysandros.' The words were husky, sounding very unlike her.

'Rio.' He said her name hoarsely, moving out of the shadows slightly, his gaze intensely focusing on her. 'If I kiss you again I might not be able to stop. I will be in danger of breaking my promise that nothing will happen unless you want it to.'

Her heart thudded. He wanted her, truly wanted her. The man she was engaged to wanted her as much as she wanted him. 'You won't be breaking that promise, Lysandros.'

Rio could scarcely believe she was saying this. Lysandros was enabling her to be the woman she really wanted to be. She wanted Lysandros to be the man she gave her virginity to and she wanted it to happen now, here—tonight.

'I want to kiss you, Rio, and so much more, but only if you really want that.' His eyes were heavy with desire, his voice soft and seductive, melting her heart a bit more. He cared. Enough to consider what she'd told him, enough to recognise how big a moment this was for her. Enough to hold back, ask if it was what she really wanted.

'I want that, Lysandros.' Her whisper cracked with emotion, ratcheting up the tension surrounding them to unbearable levels. 'I want you to kiss me.' She faltered briefly, biting her lower lip, unused to admitting how she really felt. 'I want more too. I want you.'

'Are you sure?' The raw desire in his voice didn't quite conceal the doubt. 'After everything you told me...'

'I have never been more certain of anything.' She stepped towards him, wanting to show him how ready for this she was, wanting to hide her innocence behind the bravado of being an experienced seductress. His desire filled her with the kind of power she'd never known, emboldening her, unlocking the woman within her. She wasn't a nervous and inexperienced woman any longer. He'd changed that. He'd given her the confidence to free the woman within her.

He stroked the backs of his fingers down her cheek and she had to fight against the urge to close her eyes, to lean into his touch. She needed to see his face, read the emotions in his eyes. 'I promise you I will take it slowly.'

Was her inexperience that obvious? Had he guessed she was a virgin? 'Take me to your bed.' It was all she could do to whisper those words as he moved so close to her his chest brushed against her breasts, heightening her state of arousal.

'First another kiss.' Before she could say anything his lips covered hers once more. His hands held her face, tilting her chin up gently, enabling his tongue to explore her, to entwine with hers, sending so much pleasure rushing around her she wondered if she'd be able to remain standing.

Soft Greek words added to the tension around them as he pulled back from her, caressing her face again. She didn't want to know what they meant. She wanted to pretend they were words of love, pretend that whatever it was happening between them was real, that she'd found her dream of a happy-ever-after.

'I need more than a kiss,' she teased, emboldened by rising desire.

A slow, lazy and incredibly sexy smile spread across his lips, lighting the darkness of his eyes, allowing her to see the depths of passion within them. Her body trembled as his gaze slid down her, making her skin tingle as if he'd touched her.

He looked up into her eyes, pulling at his bow tie, letting it fall to hang down, giving him that roguish appeal she hadn't realised until now could be so erotic. Then he pulled off his jacket, dropping it behind him, still without breaking that powerful eye contact.

She had the urge to move closer, to reach up and spread her hands over his chest, to unbutton the white shirt and reveal his body to her. She knew how muscled it was from their time on the yacht, knew how it felt to press herself against it as the sea had formed the only barrier between them. Now she wanted to feel every contour, to explore him so that she could remember this moment for ever.

'If you want me to, I will do far more than kiss you,' he said as he moved towards her, passion making him suddenly more dominant. She backed away until she met the keyboard of the piano, the keys jangling in discord as her palms pressed them as if she'd never played a note before in her life. It made her conscious that her inexperienced body would be as much out of tune, that she was floundering in a sea of passion. Tasting the desire in the air, she bit her bottom lip, sure she was about to drown at any moment.

Lysandros moved a little closer, and embarrassed by her moment of hesitation, she moved to him, wrapping her arms around his neck, curling her fingers into his thick hair as she looked up at him. No words were needed as she looked into his eyes before kissing him, forgetting her innocence, her fears and demanding so much more from him than just a kiss.

He took her in his arms, a strange and wild tune playing as he moved her back against the keys, his kiss answering her demands instantly. In a flash of panic she remembered that Hans had done exactly this. It almost doused the passion. Almost. Until she reassured herself. *This is right, what I want and so perfect.* And it was right. It was perfect, and it was writing over that terrible moment, erasing it for ever.

Lysandros deepened this kiss, sliding one side of her dress down off her shoulder, the tape attached to prevent her exposing herself inadvertently now completely ineffective against his demands. Her nipple hardened, her breast bare as he kissed a trail slowly down her throat then torturously slowly down her breast. She let go of him, grabbing at the piano, arching herself towards him as he took her hardened nipple in his mouth. It was pure ecstasy, so intense she almost couldn't take it.

'Lysandros.' She gasped his name out, her breathing ragged with heady need.

He looked up at her with desire-hazed eyes. 'Do you want me to stop?'

She shook her head.

'Is it nice?'

'So nice.' She didn't even recognise her husky whisper. Her whole body was on fire, needing him, needing his kiss, his touch. She was losing control, losing the ability to think as her body demanded the satisfaction she knew instinctively only he could give her.

'If I go too fast, tell me.' His gaze held hers for a moment before his hand slid down her side, over her thigh, his lips returning to torment her nipple.

There was no way she wanted him to stop now. She drew in a breath of ecstasy as with alarming ease he gathered up the silk of the skirt, his hand spreading over her bare thigh. The touch was exquisite, but it wasn't enough. She wanted more. Much more. As he moved higher, finding the lace of her panties and sliding his fingers over the delicate fabric, she thought she might explode with pleasure. Now in her head the fast and wild notes of the third movement played, driving her to further heights of pleasure.

'Lysandros,' she gasped again, almost unable to speak, not wanting the moment to end. 'Don't stop.'

While his hand continued the tormenting

exploration of lace, his lips moved away from her breast, the air cool on her skin, damp from his kiss. He looked at her with heavy eyes as she fought to keep hers open. His touch at the apex of her thighs was light and teasing, almost where she needed it but not quite.

'You are so beautiful,' he said softly, his accent deeper and more pronounced than ever.

She couldn't form any words, couldn't tell him that he made her feel beautiful as his fingers slid along the line of her panties, touching her where she craved it. She closed her eyes as he teased her, the only barrier to his touch the lace. Fire leapt within her and she moved against him instinctively, but still it wasn't enough.

Through a fog of need she looked at him, imploring him without words. She gasped in pleasure as his fingers pushed aside the material. The keys of the piano sounded again as she moved against his touch, opening her legs, feeling him going deeper as she looked into his eyes. She wanted to close her eyes, give herself up to the pleasure of what he was doing. At the same time she wanted to fight it so that it didn't have to end.

'Rio.' The gravelly whisper of her name was followed by words of Greek.

A wave of pleasure so powerful she had to close her eyes washed over her. She shuddered as he took her to the dizzying heights of orgasm, gasping his name and clutching at the piano. Slowly she became aware of his touch again, aware of her skirt dropping back down as he took her in his arms, holding her tightly against him. Kissing her hair.

He was thinking only of her pleasure, holding himself back, and her heart filled with love for him. She clung to him, savouring the moment, but her body still hummed with need, still rang with desire. She wanted him to feel the same pleasure. She wanted to touch every part of him, send him to the stars, just as he had done to her.

'Take me to your bed,' she whispered against his neck as she kissed him, the new growth of stubble prickling her lips.

As the pulse of desire thumped through him, Lysandros took Rio's hand, leading her away from the piano, across the wooden floors to his bedroom. Any misgivings about what they were doing, any doubts after her revelation, had vanished as she'd gasped out his name. There was now only one conclusion that could come of this evening. Rio would be his in every way possible.

Not just as a woman he'd made love to but as his fiancée. The thought filled him with a new emotion. He'd never felt this way before, never had that undeniable connection with any woman, as if his heart and soul were committed to hers for evermore. Unable to deal with that stark realisation with desire firing through him, he pushed it aside. Now was not the time for analysing.

His bedroom was bathed in soft light from the glow of the city and he wanted to see her naked on his bed as that light caressed her. He turned to face her as she stood by his bed, the innocence that always shone from her now muted by the desire still simmering beneath the surface, waiting for release.

He rested his hands on her hips, drawing her gently to him, smiling that she'd restored order to her dress, once again concealing the swell of her breasts from him—just.

'I want you to make love to me, Lysandros. I want to be yours.' She brushed her lips provocatively over his before looking up at him. Her beautiful eyes were so full of desire and emotion there was no longer any doubt in his mind of what she wanted.

'Rio, I want you so very much.' He kissed her, unable to restrain the passion and desire she roused in him any longer, but he remained gentle, wanting to keep the pace slow.

His fingers found the zip at her waist and slid it down as he indulged in the pleasure of her kiss. The fury of fiery passion consuming him once more, he pushed down each shoulder of the dress. He stood back, drinking her in as it slipped to the floor in a pool of indigo blue at her stiletto-clad feet.

He crouched before her, reaching up to pull the lace panties down her long legs. She clutched her fingers in his hair, stepping out of them as he kissed up her thigh, the tension in her fingers as she gripped tighter almost too much. He wanted to push her back onto the bed and plunge himself deep into her, but this was about her pleasure, not his.

Thankful he was still dressed, he continued to explore her thighs with kisses. He wanted to taste her and resumed where he'd left off at the piano. She gasped in pleasure, pulling at his hair as his tongue swirled against her, threatening to tip her over the edge once more. He took her almost to that edge again and then stood up in front of her, discarding his clothes, watching her breathe hard with passion, her desire-laden eyes locked with his.

Almost too late he remembered the necessary protection and opened a drawer behind him. He might be about to make their engagement far more of a reality than either of them had anticipated, but he had no intention of taking it further and creating a family.

Rio moved towards him, brushing her breasts against him as he tore open the foil packet. He rolled on the condom as he looked at her, then took her in his arms, kissing her as he moved her back towards the bed. Together they fell onto its softness, his body covering hers, her legs wrapping around him.

He'd wanted to take it slowly, to touch her, kiss her until neither of them could wait any longer, but as she lifted her hips, her legs pulling him to her, he lost all power of control, thrusting in deep and hard.

She cried out and stilled, her fingernails digging into his back. As questions raced for answers in his mind she moved, taking him deeper inside her, kissing his shoulders, and that final shred of control broke.

In a frenzied and wild dance that was anything but the gentle seduction he'd planned, his world splintered, her cries of ecstasy filling the room. She clung to him as her release claimed her, her legs wrapped tightly around him, keeping him deep inside her. It was so different from any other time, more intense, more powerful. Was that because he'd taken her virginity or because, despite everything, she was reaching a part of him long since closed off?

He didn't want to think of either of those scenarios right now. Instead he held her close and gave in to the need to close his eyes.

Rio lay in Lysandros's arms as darkness became day. She'd woken to feel the heavy weight of his relaxed body against hers. What had happened between them tonight had been totally magical. The pleasure of becoming his, of giving herself to him, had finally chased away those terrible nightmares, and she knew, without doubt, she was in love with Lysandros. She wasn't sure if he loved her, but did that really matter when they had a connection as powerful as this? Surely she had enough love for both of them?

He moved sleepily and she propped herself up on one elbow to look at him. The man she loved. Unable to resist the temptation, she kissed his lips, stirring him from his slumber, and with a suddenness that made her cry out he turned her onto her back and kissed her, his aroused body pressed against hers. Feeling wicked with the power she had over him, she ran her hands down his back and over his buttocks.

'Minx,' he said as he pulled himself away from her, throwing back the sheet. He went to the drawers and took out the packet of condoms, taking one and placing the box on the table next to the bed. Unable to take her eyes from him, she watched as he rolled the condom on.

Again he spoke in Greek as he crawled across the bed, kissing any part of her body he could as she laughed. Last night she'd done two things she'd thought would be impossible. Played the piano again and given herself to the man she loved. He'd been so gentle, so caring, thinking only of her. There was no way she could deny it any longer. She loved Lysandros.

Now she intended to enjoy being physically loved by him for as long as possible. Before reality crept back in.

CHAPTER NINE

AFTER AN EXQUISITE night of pleasure, making love with Lysandros, Rio had slept far later than normal. When she'd woken, she had expected Lysandros to be making excuses and stepping back from her, but the day had continued in the same passion-fuelled and romantic way of the previous night. Now, as the sun set over Athens, she sat on the roof terrace, a glass of wine in her hand and the man she knew for certain she was hopelessly in love with at her side.

'I'm sorry you weren't able to tell me about what had happened.' Lysandros's deep voice cut through her thoughts, his mind clearly on her revelation last night.

Last night, as she'd given herself to him, making her completely his, she'd known he'd guessed the truth, that it had been her first time. She hadn't told him the full details of what Hans had done to her, but at least now

Lysandros knew he hadn't taken from her the one thing she'd been saving for the right man. The one thing she'd wanted to give Lysandros, leaving him in no doubt she'd been ready to be his all those weeks ago at the recital.

Was he angry she'd been unable to tell him she was a virgin? After telling him about Hans, it hadn't felt right to tell him that too.

He took her hand, leaning across from his chair. 'Why didn't you tell me?' he coaxed gently, that caring and protective touch still there. There was a new softness in his eyes and she hated herself for hoping there could be something good between them developing—something permanent.

'Admitting what Hans had done was hard.' She lowered her gaze briefly before looking back into his classically handsome features. She could so easily believe this was real, but she had to remember only the passion and desire were real. Their engagement wasn't real or intended to be long term. It was all about giving Xena the happiness and security she needed to recover her memory. And once she did, it would end.

'Not that, Rio. I can understand completely how hard that was, but why couldn't you tell me it was your first time?' She could see a hint of sadness in his gaze. Was it regret? Would he have slept with her if he'd known she was a virgin?

She sipped her wine, desperate to distract herself as his fingers caressed her hand so lovingly. If she thought her own emotional barriers were down then so were his. This was the real Lysandros, but could she keep him with her? Prevent him from retreating behind them once more?

'You normally date experienced women. I didn't think you'd want anything to do with a twenty-five-year-old virgin. I'd already made one big revelation.' She wanted to add how he'd made her feel, how she'd fallen in love with him, but held back. Such an admission would make her more vulnerable than ever.

'I wanted it to be special for you, after what you'd told me, but if I had known you were a virgin, I would have been gentler, far more considerate.'

Rio closed her eyes, her heart flipping over. He was saying all the right things, looking at her in the right way, even caressing her hand gently as he spoke. He was doing and saying everything she would want from the man who loved her. But the sensible part of her knew there could never really be a future with him.

He didn't want to settle down and certainly didn't want to fall in love. She was just part of the plan to help Xena. To him last night was another brief affair.

She opened her eyes and looked into his, her breath catching as desire swirled in his once more. 'It was special. And you were considerate,' she whispered.

'I am honoured that after all you've been through, it was me you chose to share in the moment you discovered the passionate woman within you.'

Lysandros took her glass of wine from her, placing it on the small table at his side, then gently pulled her to her feet as he too stood up. Her heart pounded so hard she could scarcely breathe, the intensity of the desire around them heavier than the humid night air.

She couldn't hold it in any longer and the truth broke free from her. 'You made me feel so special, so desired and loved. Last night made me forget.'

'I don't know how you can possibly forget the moment a man betrays your trust like that.' The anger in his voice only added to the tension in the air.

'It's hard to forget, but I don't want it in my thoughts. I will not allow that moment, that man, to define who I am, what I feel.' Her words sounded strong, her breathing rapid and shallow, but it was the expression on his face that obliterated that memory from the past, enabling her to finally move forward.

'Nothing bad will happen to you now. I will make sure of that.'

Rio searched his eyes as questions rang through her mind. Was he offering to look after her? Help her move forward and leave the past well behind and truly find the woman she'd been last night? Did that mean he wanted their engagement to be as real as everything they'd shared last night?

Hope flared to life within her. She was under no illusions that this man would ever love her, but as her own love for him was growing, she hoped he felt something, affection that would keep them together. If he could, then maybe there was a future for them.

She'd opened her soul to him, told him her dark secret. She didn't want any more untruths between them. Boldly she looked at him, determined to change the direction of the conversation, to find out more about the man who was now her fiancé—an arrangement she wished was entirely real.

'Last night, because of you, I got past the

barriers that had prevented me from playing a single note on the piano since the night of the attack. I let go of a painful memory when I kissed you and asked you to take me to your bed.' Her voice wavered as the emotion of the moment he'd taken her by the hand and led her away from the piano rushed back. 'I wanted you to make love to me. I wanted you to be my first lover.' She looked at him cautiously. She needed to say something to make him see there could be something between them other than a temporary arrangement. 'It's liberating to come out from behind emotional barriers, Lysandros. Maybe you should try it.'

He brushed his fingers over her cheek just as he had done last night and the slow, steady thump of passion began to pump around her once more. 'And what barriers am I hiding behind?' Humour lingered sexily in his voice, a smile on his lips.

'You were nearly married. You must have really loved her to be so adamant you will not give any other woman your love again.'

His eyes hardened and the smile slipped away. Whether he admitted it or not, she had touched the demons of his past. 'Yes, Kyra and I nearly married.' Bitterness filled his voice. 'It is not something I ever think about and certainly doesn't have any lasting effects on me.'

'I'm not sure Xena shares that view.' Instantly she regretted her words. Xena believed he'd locked his heart away, shut himself out of reach of love, and hoped he and Rio would find love together. How could they? When their engagement was nothing more than a sham?

Lysandros looked at Rio's beautiful face, the setting sun casting a glow on her skin that was incredibly sexy. He stopped stroking the softness of her skin. Until she'd brought up his past he'd been hungry for her, wanting only to take her back to his bed. Now the ghosts of the past had emerged like shadows of the night, challenging him, despite what he'd just claimed. They challenged the way he felt about Rio, the way he wanted to protect and care for her. The shadows darkened. He was still the man Kyra's deception and rejection had made him. Still the man who couldn't open his heart, allowing in a woman's love, and he certainly wasn't ready to love her in return.

If only things had been different. If it had been Rio he'd fallen in love with and proposed to for real. Would he now have had the happy home life he had been desperate to avoid ever since the betrayal of his first love? Was it possible that he'd already have produced the grandchildren his mother still yearned for? Guilt stabbed at him. He was going to disappoint his mother all over again.

The gentleness of Rio's eyes coaxed the past even further from the darkness, and though their engagement would only last until Xena's memory returned, he *could* envisage more. Rio had opened up to him, told him all that had happened to her, so it was only fair that he bare his inner soul too.

'I was foolish enough to believe I had found love, to believe that Kyra and I would be together for ever.' His words were sharper than he'd intended, but the gentleness in Rio's eyes, waiting patiently for him to continue, eased the shame of admitting his male pride had got it wrong. The same pride Rio had attacked when she'd stood him up after the recital.

Rio dragged in a sharp breath, snagging his attention as she bit at her lower lip. 'That doesn't mean you can't fall in love again.'

He saw the hope in her eyes. Was she hoping to be the woman who changed that, changed him? It could never happen. He never wanted to be that vulnerable again. His childhood had made him cautious with his emotions and Kyra's betrayal had only confirmed his long-held belief it was easier, safer not to feel, not to get emotionally involved.

He must smother Rio's hopes. 'I can cope with the fact that maybe Kyra didn't want to marry me, that maybe she just got dragged along with things, but what I can't get past is the fact that she lied to me, that she was un-faithful.' He took a deep breath. Damn it. He *was* coming out from behind his barriers. 'My father was unfaithful to my mother. He de-stroyed their marriage. Our family. My faith in love.'

'I had no idea,' Rio whispered, her face pal-ing with shock.

'That's why I don't want emotion. Why I don't want love in my life. Why I *can't* love anyone.'

And you almost changed that, but I can't let you.

Rio placed her hand on his arm, her head tilting to one side, her eyes looking beseech-ingly into his. She might have held back im-portant facts, but he knew she could never lie, knew she was a woman he could trust, allow into his heart. He wanted to. What he felt for her was deeper than mere passion. Last night had been about more than just sex; that was why it had been so different for him. Yet the past clung, like a web spun in the moonlight, and only the brightest sunshine could free him.

'Kyra treated you terribly,' she whispered, making shame rush over him as he thought about all she'd been through. She'd survived the ordeal of being not only physically violated but emotionally too. 'And your father, I'm sorry.'

'I'm sure Xena has told you I haven't had a serious relationship in many years,' he said lightly, wanting to downplay the heaviness of the conversation, needing to extinguish that hope in Rio's eyes.

'She has, yes.' She smiled, her lips parting in that inviting way, sending the hum of lust hurtling around him once more. 'She had hoped we would start a long-term romance.'

There was laughter in her voice, and despite himself, he couldn't help but smile. 'And that is why she believed our engagement.'

Sadness filled Rio's eyes. He'd achieved his aim. 'But she will remember soon.'

'She will, yes,' he said as he drew her closer to him. 'But for now let's enjoy tonight.'

He brushed his lips over hers, smothering the soft sigh of pleasure. Instantly the lust in his body increased and he wanted to sweep her into his arms, carry her from the roof terrace, back to bed.

'Our last night in Athens,' she whispered between kisses.

He'd never spoken his mind like that since the disaster of his first engagement, had never allowed a woman close enough to scale the defence he'd always had around him. His instinct was to deflect her from the truth of those words as well as prevent himself from analysing them. Instead he allowed desire to carry him out of the shadows of the past, making him realise he needed more nights with Rio, more passion, more desire. 'But not our last night ever.'

The hope that had started to grow within Rio burst open like a flower in the morning sunshine as the full impact of his words washed over her. He might not have said anything about loving her, but he still wanted her, wanted this moment. He believed whatever it was that had sparked to life between them was a good thing—for now at least.

'You want more nights like this?' she asked shyly, conscious of his body against hers, the way he caressed her face and the heavy look

202 SEDUCING HIS CONVENIENT INNOCENT

of desire in his eyes. There was no mistaking that there would be many amazing nights of passion ahead of them in this convenient engagement. Maybe it could one day lead somewhere else, perhaps be the beginning of much deeper and more meaningful things.

'We have something good, Rio. It proves that the misguided sentiment of love is not needed between us.'

'It's not?' She knew the smile had slipped from her face, even before she saw his frown.

'We are attracted to one another and the chemistry between us is nothing short of hot. Love would only complicate that.' That last sentence was said with conviction and the flame of hope within her heart spluttered slightly, as if a big gust of wind had raced across the roof terrace.

'Love always complicates things,' she said, quashing down any notion that one day he might love her as she now loved him. 'It will be different when we are back on the island with Xena.'

'In that case, we need to make the most of our last night here in Athens—alone.'

'Just what do you have in mind?' She was determined to do exactly that, to lose herself in the dream of love for one more night. Power raced through her as she teased him and, emboldened, she moved against him.

'Temptress,' he growled, his lips claiming hers in a kiss far more demanding and forceful than any of last night. She'd done this to him, pushed his legendary control to the limit, and that knowledge filled her with power, with excitement. 'What is it you want, Rio?'

Rio looked at him, her heart beating so loudly she was sure it echoed around them. His dark eyes watched her intently, waiting for her to say something.

'Another night with you,' she whispered huskily.

'Then you leave me no option,' he said, whisking her off her feet before striding across the roof terrace.

She feigned resistance, wriggling in his arms and laughing at the same time. She'd never been so happy, so carefree. She was going to make the most of this final night, allow herself to believe he loved her one final time.

As that thought lingered temptingly, she lay on the bed as his body covered hers, his kiss intoxicating and demanding. She met his passion head-on, losing herself in this bubble of happiness in which she now found herself. It didn't matter what happened tomorrow, next week or next year. All that mattered right now was that she was in the arms of the man she loved. She might not be able to tell him she loved him, but her body could—and tonight she intended to do exactly that.

CHAPTER TEN

ON THEIR RETURN to the island Rio had found it easier than before to create the illusion she and Lysandros were in love. Xena still hadn't recovered any memories but fully bought into the romance of their engagement. Once Lysandros had left for Athens Rio had faced a barrage of questions from Xena, but, not wanting to say exactly what had happened between them after the charity ball, she had been evasive in her details of the weekend away. Xena's satisfied expression proved she knew it had been a weekend for lovers. Were her deepening feelings of love for Lysandros that obvious?

In just two days Lysandros was due to return to his sister's villa for the family engagement party Xena had been planning. Rio was nervous. How should she act around him in front of his family? Would his desire for her have run its course or would he want more nights with her?

'You miss him, don't you?' Xena's voice interrupted her doubts and questions. She pushed them aside, focusing instead on Lysandros's impending return. Just knowing she would see him again very soon filled her tummy with butterflies, making her heart flutter.

'We have just got engaged.' Rio tried valiantly to answer Xena's question without admitting the truth. 'Of course I miss him.'

She missed what they'd shared for those couple of nights in Athens. Not just the intimacy and the passion of their lovemaking but the gentleness he'd shown her, the way he'd cared about her, his concern for her as they'd arrived at his apartment. That night, as she'd touched the piano and met his gaze, it had been as if he'd known, even before she'd told him the truth, exactly how hard it had been to do that, let alone play.

'You've fallen for him, haven't you? Really fallen for him.' Xena laughed, a sound so in contrast to her thoughts it made Rio feel even more anxious.

'Isn't that what people do when they get engaged?' Rio kept her voice light, determined not to show the depth of her feelings—her love.

'I knew all along you two were so right for each other.' Xena grinned, smug satisfaction on her face, her dark eyes sparkling, so like her brother's on the rare occasion he let his guard down. 'When did you make up, by the way?'

'Make up?' Rio feigned ignorance, despite the implications of that question.

'I can't recall why,' Xena began again. 'Not yet at least, but I do remember you had broken it off with him.'

'You remember something?' Rio was so pleased. Xena was recovering and her smile was full of excitement. 'Do you remember anything else?'

'I'm not sure,' Xena replied. 'But now it's started to come back, I'm sure I will begin to remember other things. That's not important now, Rio. You and Lysandros are. When did you get back together?'

'At the hospital. After your accident,' Rio said cautiously. 'It was the first time we had seen each other.' It was in part true. She and Lysandros had shared something special before Hans had spoilt it. Rio said nothing else, knowing it would be all too easy to give away the truth of their reconciliation, expose the fake engagement. If Xena's memory was slowly coming back, she didn't want to risk upsetting that, even though she would soon know the truth.

'There's something,' Xena said, a frown on her face. 'I can't quite recall it.'

'What is it about? The accident? Do you remember something new?'

As soon as she'd asked the questions, seen Xena's expression change, Rio worried she would remember everything. What Hans had done. The argument with Ricardo. The accident.

When she'd returned from Athens it had been to find Xena was much more the woman she'd been before she'd fallen for Ricardo. Before the time she'd admitted he was married. A time that had almost torn apart their friendship as Rio had tried to warn her friend that getting involved with a married man could only mean heartache and disaster. She'd never anticipated the scale of that heartache and had no idea why Lysandros shouldn't know anything about Ricardo.

Should she tell Xena he now knew? No. She wasn't even sure if Xena recalled her relationship with Ricardo.

Xena sighed wistfully. 'Everything that has happened, the accident, my loss of memory, will be worth it when you and Lysandros finally set the date. It's what I'd always hoped for.'

'Xena Drakakis, if I didn't know better, I'd say that you had planned this.' Rio laughed at the mock wounded expression on her friend's face.

'Yes, I had always wanted you two together.' Her tone changed, and she looked down guiltily. 'But now I am starting to recall things.'

If Xena's memory returned fully, it would end the engagement. Lysandros had made that all too clear. She would lose the man she loved. Rio's heart was tearing apart—for herself and for Xena.

'Xena?' Rio questioned gently.

'I can remember other things, Rio. I can remember why you ended the relationship.'

'You can?' Rio tentatively asked.

'Yes, I can. It was what Hans did, wasn't it? The attack? That's why you ended things with Lysandros.'

Rio gulped, unable to say anything. It was all over now. Xena's memory was returning. The fog her friend had lived in since the accident was lifting.

'It was.' Rio finally spoke.

Xena shook her head, disappointment clear

on her face. 'I didn't tell him why, but I do remember telling him to give you the space you needed. I warned him not to contact you. So, what happened? Are you really engaged to him? Did you two get back together, get engaged, purely to help me regain my memory?'

Rio was sure her mouth must be gaping open in shock. Xena had guessed their plan, had guessed she and her brother were acting out a fake engagement. What was she supposed to do now? Tell Xena the truth? How could she do that when all along her friend had wanted to see her brother happily married, and now that he'd told her about the marriage he'd almost made, she could understand where Xena's desire for that had come from. But did Xena realise he didn't want love in his life? That he couldn't love her, couldn't love anyone?

There was only one thing for it. Tell Xena the truth. 'I'm sorry, Xena; we thought if you were surrounded by happiness, it would help you recover—from the accident and the amnesia.'

'It did.' Xena looked so vulnerable Rio's heart went out to her. 'But you must feel something for him to get engaged?'

She owed Xena the truth. Owed herself the truth.

'I had been falling for Lysandros before I ended it. So much so that I couldn't face him after what had happened.'

'Hans?' Xena said sharply, making Rio look at her. She couldn't verbally acknowledge that so just nodded. 'And now? Do you love Lysandros now?'

'I do, yes.' She wouldn't tell Xena that Lysandros had said he could never love anyone again. That heartbreaking bit of information was something she didn't want Xena knowing.

'It's hard, isn't it?' Xena said softly, looking down at the floor, unable to meet Rio's gaze, but when she did, tears filled her eyes. 'I love Ricardo. I should never have run out on him like I did the night of the accident. He wanted time. He and his wife were separating; their marriage had fallen apart long before he first took me out. She even knows about me.'

Rio was stunned. Xena remembered everything.

'What do you want to do about Ricardo?' Rio asked gently, relieved the attention had slipped away from her and Lysandros. She sat next to Xena, who was making a brave attempt at holding back tears. Maybe she did need to cry. Maybe she did need to let out the pain of her broken heart.

Xena looked at her with big, wide, tearful eyes. 'I spoke to him yesterday.'

She'd contacted him? Yesterday? 'Did that help?'

'He and his wife have filed for divorce. He wants to see me, Rio.' The hope echoing in Xena's voice was the same hope Rio had clung to as she'd lain in Lysandros's arms after they'd made love the first time—and each time afterwards.

'If it's what you want, Xena, I will do whatever I can to make it happen for you.'

Rio knew the pain of loving someone so much it hurt. She recognised that pain in Xena's eyes.

'Thank you,' Xena whispered, sitting taller as if finding strength from somewhere. 'But first we have an engagement to celebrate.'

'You just told me you know none of it is real.' Rio's mind whirled. How could Xena possibly want her and Lysandros to continue with the engagement now?

'He is besotted with you, Rio. He watches every move you make. I've seen him doing it. There is no way I'm going to allow you two to go your separate ways again.' A new determination filled Xena's voice, but surely she realised there were some things even Xena couldn't make happen?

'We can't stay engaged, Xena. Not now.' The declaration was out before she could stop it.

'Of course you can. Everything is planned. Family invited. You are engaged, Rio. To be married—to my brother.' The enthusiasm in Xena's voice couldn't quell the anxiety bubbling inside her.

'It's not possible, Xena.' Desperation filled Rio's voice and she wondered if she was trying to convince herself or Xena.

'You just told me you love him.' Xena spoke softly, her hand reaching out, touching Rio's arm in a reassuring gesture, her expression brighter now she was smiling once again. 'That's what you said, isn't it?'

'Yes, I did.' Rio couldn't keep it in. 'I love Lysandros.'

'Then there is nothing more to discuss. In two days' time we will officially celebrate your engagement and I'll be making sure he sets the date. Nothing would make me happier than for you to be my sister-in-law.'

Impatient to see Rio again, Lysandros had left the office at an unusually early hour, making his assistant smile as he'd claimed to be testing out another of his yachts. Were his feelings for Rio that transparent?

He'd arrived far earlier than planned after enjoying the freedom of the sea. As he'd neared the villa he'd heard, through the open doors onto the terrace, his sister and Rio talking, but he hadn't been able to make out exactly what they were saying. By the time he reached the terrace their words had become clearer.

'You just told me you love him.'

Rio loved him?

He stood on the terrace of the villa, trying to take in what he'd just heard Xena say, what he'd just heard Rio reply.

'Yes, I did. I love Lysandros.'

He'd thought himself hardened, immune to such emotions, but replayed again and again those words inside his head. Rio loved him? He had tried to convince Rio what he felt for her was just desire. Heated lust borne out of several nights of passion. Now he needed to convince himself. He didn't want it to be something stronger—something far more destructive.

He didn't want to fall in love with his convenient and temporary fiancée. The woman who was now playing out the role to perfection, claiming how much she loved him so that Xena wouldn't question their fake engagement.

Of course, that was it. She hadn't meant it at all. She didn't love him. It had been for Xena's benefit.

Relief surged through him. He could never be that vulnerable again. He didn't want to love anyone. He didn't want to lower the barriers he'd strategically built around himself, open himself to the kind of hurt and pain he'd known more than once in the past. He didn't want to risk that pain again, that rejection and devastation of trust.

Should he turn and go? The thought hung in the air as Xena laughed in delight and he could almost imagine her hugging Rio. 'You will be my sister.'

He didn't turn and go. Instead he walked into the villa, Rio and Xena springing apart, Rio's face ashen white.

'She would also be my wife,' he said as he moved into the room to stand by the large grand piano occupying the centre of the vast space. His voice was brusque, but Xena grinned up at him. She really was invested in their engagement. He'd have to make out he and Rio wanted a long engagement if Xena didn't start recovering her memory soon. The problem would then be that being around Rio for much longer would test him—test his vow never to become emotionally involved again. But he'd do it for Xena.

In a bid to release the tension suddenly in the air, he ruffled his sister's hair, knowing full well she hated it, and when she squealed in protest, he laughed. At that exact moment he made eye contact with Rio and it happened all over again. The spark ignited. The strong pull of attraction, so intense he had no option but to go to her. The sensation his heart was overflowing with the kind of emotion he'd never wanted tore through him again.

Oblivious to Xena's teasing words, he went to Rio. The woman who filled his dreams with heated memories, something no other woman had ever done.

'Lysandros?' There was a question in his name as she spoke softly. Was she trying to second-guess the next move they made or was she aware he'd just heard her declaration of love? A declaration he could believe or dismiss as part of the act.

'The Greek sunshine is enhancing your beauty. Giving you a healthy glow,' he said, taking her hand, raising her fingertips to his lips, pressing a kiss onto her slender fingers. It was all he could do to stop himself from remembering how they had caressed the keys of his piano when she'd finally played again. Then much later, as they'd lain in bed, how they had caressed his body. He could still feel her soft teasing touch on his chest, the slow lingering trail she'd made down over his stomach before touching him in a way that had driven him wild.

Enough. He pushed the memory aside, fighting with the words he'd just heard Rio say, aware his sister was watching every move he made.

Xena sighed as she sat back down. 'This is so perfect.'

Was it perfect? To be loved by a woman he didn't want to love, a woman he didn't want to occupy his heart? He needed to be alone with Rio, needed to know what her true reactions were, her true feelings. She must have been saying those words to Xena as part of the act, part of the deal he'd made with her. Exactly what he'd expect her to do, so why was that so unsettling?

Because you are falling in love with her. Despite everything you told her, you are falling in love with her.

He gritted his teeth against the knowledge he'd almost made a fool of himself. Almost believed the words he'd overheard Rio saying as part of her role play and exposed his growing vulnerability, his growing weakness.

'You two should spend some time alone. Take a romantic stroll on the beach.' There was mischief in Xena's voice, showing she was finally more her usual bubbly self. The Xena he knew so well was beginning to come back.

'Shall we take a walk?' He didn't miss the look of worry crossing Rio's face.

'I'd like that.' Her words were barely above a whisper, her face pale beneath the newly gained tan.

Together they walked along the sand until they were alone, and it was several minutes before she spoke hesitantly. 'Have you ever wondered if Xena might have guessed our engagement isn't real?'

'Our engagement is real. You are wearing my ring.' The words snapped from him and those beautiful eyes widened in surprise.

'But…' Rio began. Lysandros wasn't in the mood for discussion about anything other than what he'd just heard.

'The reason is different, that's all.' He cut across her words as emotions assailed him, bombarding him and pushing him out of his safety zone. 'I heard you and Xena talking just now.'

She didn't look at him, didn't even stop walking.

Damn her. Was she going to make him say it? 'You were telling her about us. You said you loved me. It was just part of the act, wasn't it? A way to convince her our engagement is real.'

She stopped, looking down at the sand, and he wished he hadn't been so harsh, but when she looked back up at him, her chin lifted in defiance. She'd become the same little spitfire he'd done battle with while Xena had lain in the hospital bed. The realisation crashed over him as if a storm had suddenly rushed in off the sea. He wanted her to love him. Hell, *he* wanted to love her.

'And does she still believe it is real?' He moved closer to her, wanting to prove how very real their engagement was beginning to be, wanting to remind her that last weekend she'd lost her virginity to him, giving him something special. If there was any chance those words he'd heard her say moments ago were real, then didn't he owe it to her to be honest? To tell her what he'd been denying since that night in Athens?

He wanted to love her, but he couldn't quite let go of the past. Just as she'd sat at the piano in his apartment, locked in her own world of regret, he too was there now.

'Yes,' Rio whispered, and he couldn't stop himself. 'She believes it's real, but it isn't. It can't ever be real—because you don't want that, you won't let me in.'

He took her in his arms, bringing her close against him, feeling as if he'd been all at sea but had now found the port he'd never known existed. He'd found the woman who could make him forget the past.

'There is nothing fake about the way I feel when I hold you.' His voice became hoarse with emotion. Rio tried to look away, but gently he tilted her chin up, whispering against her lips, 'Neither is there anything false about this.'

The kiss was so powerful it totally consumed him. Her response was instant, her arms wrapping around his neck, her delicious body against his. It was paradise and as it ended he took her hand, beginning to walk slowly along the beach again.

She pulled away from him. 'It's real, yes, but it's just desire. Nothing more.' She hesitated. 'If… When Xena knows, we must end this. Stop this charade of being engaged—before it goes too far.'

'When she remembers, yes, we will.' He let her go, stepping away from her. Xena didn't remember yet, and until she remembered, he and Rio could continue to indulge in their desire. But what about that night in Athens? What about the heated passion that had filled that whole weekend? Was it really as she now claimed? Nothing more than desire? 'We need to talk to Xena.'

'And if she remembers?' Rio looked at him, worry startlingly clear in her eyes.

'Then we can end the engagement, but she has to tell us. We can't say anything, can't raise any questions over our relationship.' Lysandros found himself hoping Xena *hadn't* remembered anything, that he and Rio would be forced to remain engaged. 'I don't want to risk upsetting her.'

As she and Lysandros returned to the villa the hope there was a chance he could one day love her, as she loved him, was finally gone. Rio had felt desire in his kiss, had seen it in his eyes, but desire wasn't enough. She had to be strong. She didn't want to be part of a one-sided love affair. As soon as he found out

Xena had regained her memory, she and Lysandros were over. And Xena had done just that. Time was ticking on their deal, on her illusion of love.

Voices sounded from inside the villa as they approached. Xena's voice and a man's. Ricardo's voice. Every nerve in Rio's body tensed. He was here? There was no escaping it now. This was the moment everything ended, the moment her heart broke.

'Xena has a visitor?' Lysandros asked, suspicion laced into every word.

Rio could feel the colour leaching from her face as she looked at Lysandros. Xena's memory was back; there was no point avoiding it. 'It's Ricardo.'

Before Rio could gather her scrambled thoughts, Lysandros marched into the villa and she rushed after him, remembering Xena's recent conversation about how she loved Ricardo. She recalled Xena saying they had spoken. Had she invited him, even knowing it would need massive explanations to her family? And worse, knowing how Lysandros would take it?

The air filled with furious Greek as he stormed into the room, Xena and Ricardo leaping apart like teenagers caught out. Rio had no idea what he was saying, what Xena was saying. It was more heated than she'd ever seen either Xena or Lysandros. This was brother and sister pitched against each other in a wild battle of words.

She couldn't let this happen. She had to stand up for Xena, even if it meant losing Lysandros—because she'd never really had him, his love. 'Stop.'

Her word rang round the room. Ricardo stepped into the spotlight, taking Xena in his arms, holding her as she tried to fight the tears.

Lysandros turned to her and Rio knew the moment of truth had come. 'What the hell is going on?'

Before she could say anything Xena had launched into the gap her silence had created. Rio stood numbly as Xena explained. How she'd remembered almost everything a few days ago and how she and Ricardo had made up, prompting him to come to the island. How she'd told Rio she knew they were pretending to be engaged, but how they *should* be.

Lysandros looked at her and Rio knew from the coldness of his eyes it was too late. She should have told him, but he'd completely shocked her by admitting he'd heard what she'd said to Xena, taking the urgency away from that as she'd tried to protect her heart. 'As you are already aware, we no longer need to keep up the pretence of being lovers—or being engaged.'

Lysandros turned to glare angrily at Ricardo, who stood his ground, looking back at him rebelliously. They remained like that for several minutes until at last Lysandros moved.

He went to his sister, taking her gently from Ricardo's arms, holding her tight, whispering in Greek, showing once again his compassion in the face of devastating news. She had no idea how long she watched the tender moment, but eventually Lysandros pulled away, returning Xena to Ricardo's embrace.

'Look after her,' he instructed Ricardo, then turned to go. 'I'm leaving.'

As he passed her he didn't even glance her way. Rio wanted to crumple to the cool marble floor, give in to the tears the whole encounter had evoked. She'd lost the man she loved.

CHAPTER ELEVEN

LYSANDROS COULDN'T BREATHE, couldn't think. Rio had known Xena's memory had returned. She'd blatantly asked him what would happen when it did, but hadn't told him. She'd kept something from him that changed everything between them. She'd deceived him.

He and Rio could really have had something special, but he'd fallen into the same trap all over again. Raw pain from the past opened up, snatching away all that he'd foolishly believed Rio was.

He couldn't stay. Couldn't look at Rio. Not when he'd finally taken down the last of his barriers. Dismantled them all—for Rio. Because he'd wanted her. Wanted to be with her. But now everything had changed.

He marched along the beach to where only a short time ago he'd kissed Rio. It was here he'd realised his heart had finally begun to open to love—her love. He wanted Rio's love, wanted to love her, wanted to share with her the emotion he'd locked out of his life for so long.

Raw and painful emotions had crashed over him as he'd heard Rio's conversation with Xena. To hear her say she loved him had confused him, shocked him. A whole range of emotions had assailed him. Finally, he'd acknowledged the truth he'd been desperately running from for the last few months.

Lysandros took in a deep breath, standing firm in the wet sand near the water's edge as the waves dragged it away from him, trying to unbalance him. It was as if the pull of the sea was forcing him to admit what he'd been avoiding all along. Right here, just a short while ago, he'd been on the brink of telling Rio how he felt, that he wanted their engagement to be real—because he was falling in love with her.

A larger wave rushed in, soaking him above his ankles, but still he didn't move. He'd already drowned, already slipped beneath the surface. It had happened the moment he'd first kissed Rio, but it had been in Athens that he'd lost the battle. That spark of attraction had fired into life, bringing love back to his heart.

Only he'd been too damned arrogant to believe it.

Now the painful truth that he'd fallen in love with a woman who, despite what he'd overheard, had ripped his heart in two. He ran his hands through his hair in agitation. Her declaration of love for him to Xena hadn't been true. She wanted the engagement over. Before it went too far.

Should he go back into the villa? Tell Rio how he felt, or be there for Xena? Who should he put first? Xena, his beloved sister? Or Rio, the woman who had just told him that their engagement was over, rendering him as vulnerable as a newborn?

If he'd been a better man, a better brother, one able to connect emotionally, none of this would have happened. The solid wall of defence he'd built around him after Kyra's betrayal had shut out his sister—and pushed Rio away.

He walked further along the beach. He couldn't go back to the villa yet. Xena had Ricardo and it was all too obvious they loved one another. Whatever he thought about the man, Ricardo would look after her. But it was the image of Rio, standing there, that filled his mind. She hadn't even been able to look at him as the truth had unfolded, hadn't said anything, hadn't tried to stop him going.

He continued walking, brisk paces through the waves as they slid onto the beach. He couldn't face Rio yet. His emotions, his heart were all too vulnerable. He needed to lock them away, put them back behind the barriers. Only then could he talk to her, end their fake engagement—their deal.

Sensations of claustrophobia overwhelmed Rio. She needed air, needed to get out of the villa. Xena and Ricardo were deep in conversation, declaring love for each other and apologising. They didn't need her. Silently she slipped out onto the terrace.

From her vantage point she saw Lysandros on the beach, striding angrily along at the water's edge. The firm set of his shoulders showed his anger. He didn't want her. Didn't need her. Xena's memory had returned and their deal was over. Whatever she felt for him, she had to shut it down.

She couldn't stay on the island now. She had to leave. But how? She was marooned here, and the only boat belonged to the man who had just walked away from her, unable to even look at her.

There was only one thing for it. She returned to the villa, avoiding Xena and Ricardo and going to her room to pack. In the kind of haste she'd watched many times in the movies, she threw her belongings into her case. Then slipped the elegant ring off her finger. Placing it on the dressing table. Xena would find it.

Thankfully Xena and Ricardo had gone when she returned to the living area, and with her heart breaking, Rio left the villa. She glanced along the beach, seeing Lysandros had walked further away. She turned in the opposite direction, heading for the jetty where he'd moored his speedboat.

It bobbed ominously on the waves as she dragged her case down the wooden jetty. She looked down at the crystal waters, the sandy seabed clear to see, along with a starfish. How could she still see something so beautiful when her world was falling apart?

'You've blown it,' she told herself as she hefted her case up and over the side of the boat, careful not to scratch it, knowing the sleek craft was new. Lysandros had taken it out on its maiden voyage last weekend when he'd brought her back to the island after their time in Athens.

How had so much changed in one week?

In Athens they'd been lovers. She'd lost her virginity and her heart to him. Now a week later and with just two days until their engagement party, they were as far from lovers as a man and woman could be. Whatever they had discovered in Athens was over. She'd known it would never last but had foolishly hoped for love. Hoped that she would be the woman to mend his heart, enable him to love again, love her.

She closed her eyes against the threatening tears, placing her hands on her hips and tilting her face up to the sun, allowing the warmth to ease her pain, her despair. She'd hoped such an action would soothe her, calm the raging storm within her, but it didn't.

Deflated and humiliated, she knelt, trying to free one of the mooring ropes at the front of the long speedboat. She had absolutely no idea what she was doing or even what she'd do once the boat was free of the ropes. All she knew was that the gleaming white craft represented freedom and escape.

Despair filled her. She couldn't even free the rope. A strangled cry of frustration tore from her as she heard footsteps, turning to see the man who now possessed her heart striding down the jetty towards her.

'If you are that desperate to leave, all you had to do was ask.' Lysandros's icy and controlled voice cut through her panic.

Damn him. Why did he have to sound so sure of himself, so in control and, worse still, so sexy?

She leapt to her feet, boldly facing him, injecting haughtiness into her voice. 'Very well. I'm asking. Will you take me to Athens?'

'You seriously want to leave? After everything that has happened between us? Everything that has been said?'

For the briefest second, he looked out of control, vulnerable, but as he stepped closer she wondered if it had been a trick of the light. His eyes sparked with anger, strengthening her resolve to protect her breaking heart, to get away.

'Yes, and that's why I want to go. I want to return to the life I should never have left. Our deal is over, Lysandros. Just as you wanted,' she snapped as frustration surged through her. All he was doing now was proving he was the wrong man for her, the kind of man who demanded everything, the kind of man unable to be emotionally open and love her. How stupid was she that she'd hoped otherwise?

'At least allow me to help you. You'll be

going nowhere until you release all the mooring ropes.' He was taunting her, but there was also firmness to his voice, anger lurking beneath the composed exterior.

Rio stared at him, completely taken aback. He obviously wanted her out of his life so much he would actually take her. Her heart broke into thousands of tiny pieces, like crystal shattering, splinters flying everywhere. There would be no hope of finding the pieces and putting them back together.

Within seconds he'd freed the sleek craft of its moorings and was aboard, starting the motor. Rio still stood on the jetty but finally roused herself into action, putting to one side the pain and hurt. She hastily jumped into the speedboat, as if her life depended on it, and sat at the very stern, as far away from Lysandros as she could get.

Seconds later the boat lurched into life and they began heading away from the island, the pace picking up over the clear waters, making them insignificant and small against the vastness of the sea.

The wind whipped at her hair, pulling the last part of her ponytail free, and Rio clutched it to the side of her neck, looking back at the island, now nothing more than a dark smudge on the horizon. Even though she felt sorry for herself, her thoughts turned to Xena. Would she be okay with Ricardo? What if he went back to his wife? The boat bounced over the water, taking her further away.

She swallowed hard against the tears threatening once more. She didn't want to show weakness. The boat slowed and she opened her eyes, looking around her as the engine died. The boat began to drift to a stop on the blue waters that surrounded them.

'Why have we stopped?' She turned to look at Lysandros stepping down from the seat and away from the controls. What was he doing? Was this the moment he told her how much he despised her, how disappointed he was and, worst of all, that he never wanted to see her again? Well, she wouldn't give him the satisfaction.

'We need to talk,' Lysandros said, balancing with ease as the boat rocked and rolled on the swell of the sea. Rio, however, looked less comfortable with the sensation, but he pressed on with the plan he'd had to rapidly form as he'd found her trying to make her escape—in his boat.

He needed to talk to her alone. He had to

know what had really happened. Right from the moment he'd kissed her in London at the recital to now. He couldn't let her go. Not like this. When he'd seen her heading to the jetty, her case rumbling behind her, he'd known that alone at sea would be the perfect place for such a discussion.

'There is nothing more to say,' she said, trying to stand but stumbling back a pace before sitting down, unused to being at sea in a smaller boat, obviously feeling every swell on the deep waters.

Her lovely hair was in disarray and her face very pale. She looked far more vulnerable and innocent than he'd ever seen her. Far more than she had appeared the night she'd played the piano in his apartment. The night he'd taken her virginity. A night that had changed everything. Changed him.

He crossed to the stern of the boat, sitting down next to her. Now was not the time to dominate. This was not a boardroom deal that required power and control of the situation. This was Rio, the woman who had penetrated his cold heart, brought love back into his life. This was also his last chance to convince her of that.

'You can't go like this. Not after everything

that has happened between us.' He thought back to Athens, to the deepening desire that had claimed them both. He couldn't allow her to walk away yet. He needed to buy himself more time. He needed to come to terms with the revelations of this afternoon.

The fact Rio had kept Xena's returned memory from him and had manipulated the situation was at total odds with his own admission of how he felt about Rio.

'I have to go, Lysandros—*because* of what has happened between us.'

Rio looked at him, her eyes begging him, pleading him to understand.

'Doesn't that night in Athens mean anything?' He wasn't ready to allow Rio to walk out of his life—again.

'It does,' Rio said, pulling her hair from her face, holding it tight to prevent the wind snatching it back. 'It means too much and that is why I *have* to go.'

Lysandros's world rocked. His inability to acknowledge his emotions, to connect emotionally with anyone, was pushing away not just Xena but Rio—the most important woman in his life. That thought shocked him.

He'd failed the people he loved, the people

who counted on him. It seemed to be what he did best.

Lysandros closed his eyes against the thought of the two women he loved dealing with so much alone. Savagely he pushed the full implications of that acknowledgement aside.

'Why does it mean you have to go, Rio?' Even as he asked the question he doubted she would give him the answer. She had well and truly locked him out of her life, her thoughts, her emotions.

'We should never have got together, Lysandros, should never have got engaged.'

Even as he asked he knew why—knew it was because of him, because he was emotionally unobtainable. Anger and guilt fused inside him, thrashing around like a raging storm.

He swore savagely in Greek as the truth lashed at him. 'I should never have forced you to become engaged—not like that, not as part of a deal.'

'You did it for Xena,' she said with conviction, forcing him to look at her, to calm the furious bubbles of anger before they spilled over. 'Because you love her.' The warmth of her touch unleashed that spark of attraction, that fatal awareness of her he couldn't deny.

'And now she too will despise me for what I've done to you. If I had known about Hans, I would never have forced you into such a deal, Rio.'

Rio jumped up, the boat steadier now, and she stood over him. 'Xena could never despise you. She might be angry, but she will never despise you.' The passion, the truth of her words was as clear as the crystal waters beneath them.

Now he knew everything. Rio had wanted to protect Xena, proving her loyalty to her friend. She'd put Xena before everything, including her own happiness.

'What about you? Do you despise me, Rio?' He stood, moving closer, his voice becoming a whisper as he fought the overload of emotions he'd never wanted to indulge in again, the kind he no longer wanted to banish from his life—but was it too late?

CHAPTER TWELVE

'DESPISE YOU?' RIO's heart thumped, hope flaring to life within her. She had to tell him. 'I meant what I said to Xena.' Lysandros watched her, saying nothing, making it even more difficult, his dark eyes searching hers. 'When I told her I loved you.'

'Was that true or was it merely part of the act of being engaged, something to make Xena believe it was real?' His voice deepened, becoming more demanding, and even though he sat next to her calmly, he still dominated the very air she breathed. His question went to the heart of the matter like an arrow to the bullseye.

Her nerves wavered in the face of his question. Had he understood what she'd said? She tried to find her courage after the admission he'd barely registered, too painfully true to make it again. 'I have told you a great many things as part of our deal, but I want you to ignore them all now. Xena has recovered her memory and I want to put this farce of an engagement behind me.'

He looked down at her hand, to the finger on which he'd placed the engagement ring such a short time ago. She remained firm, watching him, mimicking the same command he exuded so naturally, trying not to remember the heady sexual tension in the air as she'd played the piano at his apartment. She shut her mind against the pleasure of giving herself so completely to him that night. There was no alternative. She had to walk away from this—from him.

'You want what we have to end?' There was hurt and accusation laced into that question, neither of which she'd ever intended to inflict on him. 'You don't want to be engaged to me?'

'No, I don't. We can't truly be together, Lysandros. We want different things, need different things from a relationship. We are too different.' He sat back from her, from her passionate outburst, thankfully giving her space, room to think, to breathe, because she couldn't do either when he was so close to her.

'Different?' He touched her face, his fingers soft against her cheek, and she couldn't help but close her eyes to the sensation. She needed to get her emotions under control, needed to find some strength from somewhere. She'd just admitted she loved him, but he had casually sidetracked her words.

'From the very beginning I always thought that for you the attraction was purely physical. That once we'd spent a night together you would want to move on to the next woman.' Rio hung on to the strength she'd found, needing to tell him everything. After all, she had nothing to lose now. She'd already lost him, lost her hope of being loved by him. 'That was why I had to be sure.' She paused, looking at him. 'Before I spent the night with you. And then when Hans did what he did, I couldn't tell you. Not after I'd finally made the decision to make our relationship physical. I just didn't feel I could.'

'I never wanted you to feel that way, Rio,' Lysandros said, taking her hand in his. 'I was shut down emotionally against feeling anything romantic. I hadn't connected emotionally with a woman for many years. That was until you walked into my life. That's when I knew I wanted more. That I wanted you.'

She thought of the afternoon at the recital. He'd seemed different from his usual self that afternoon. More intense. But, then, she had been too. She'd been about to tell him she wanted to be with him all night.

'Me?' she asked, needing to know. Was Lysandros saying he'd envisaged more from their relationship than just a brief affair?

'Yes, you, Rio. At first it was only Xena who saw what we could be, that there was something special between us. I was still too locked up behind my protective wall, but that afternoon at the recital I realised she was right.'

'It would never have worked, though, Lysandros. I couldn't be the kind of woman you wanted, the kind you normally dated,' she whispered, her heart and soul being dragged out into the sunshine, laid bare before him.

'It's because you weren't the kind of woman I usually dated that I saw there was a future for us.' He smiled in that devastatingly sexy way she loved so much.

She had no idea what he was trying to tell her. No idea what the outcome of this conversation would be. All she knew was she had told him she loved him, and not once had he mentioned that word to her. He was doing all he could to avoid it.

She didn't say anything. She couldn't. Instead she allowed the motion of the boat to soothe her.

'In the hospital, you made it clear you only wanted me in Greece because I could help Xena recover,' she whispered, shocked to realise she'd spoken her thoughts aloud.

'I know.' He looked into her eyes, his own so dark she couldn't fathom out the emotion in them. He was the one hiding secrets now. 'I'm sorry.'

'What happens now?' She lifted her chin, looking directly at him, giving him the opportunity to be honest. To say they were over or to say he wanted her in his life—because he loved her. She didn't need an engagement or marriage. All she needed was him, his love.

'I want this engagement to end,' Lysandros said firmly, seeing raw emotions fill Rio's eyes. He should just say it, just tell her, but still he found it difficult. Letting go of years of caution wasn't easy.

'Then we both want the same thing.' Rio's voice faltered. 'To end the engagement.'

'I want you, Rio. You cannot deny you are as attracted to me as I am to you.' The air crackled as she looked up at him. His heart was pounding like a drum as he waited, cursing inwardly that he still couldn't tell her just how much he wanted her.

'It's true. I do want you,' she said in a resigned voice. 'But I want more than that, Lysandros. Much more. I don't want to pretend any more.'

'I'm not pretending, Rio. I want you. I want more too.'

She looked up at him and in the depths of her brown eyes he saw nothing but sadness. 'Want isn't enough.'

Was she going to force him to lay bare his heart? His emotions? Why couldn't he say it? What was holding him back? He cursed Kyra and her wicked lies, even cursed Rio's loyalty to his sister, which had played into all his doubts.

'Want is a good place to start.'

'No. Nothing is going to start. I need to go home. Now, please, Lysandros.' The firm determination in her voice was clearer than ever, but he wasn't going to give up. If he had to lay his heart on the line, he'd do it. He wanted Rio to stay, wanted what they'd had in Athens.

'I want you to stay.' Damn it. What was stopping him from telling her how he really felt?

'I can't,' she whispered, moving away from

him. He could see tears threatening in her eyes and knew he had to prove to her how he felt or lose her for ever.

'Want isn't enough.' That was what she had said. Would his love be enough?

He took a deep breath, unlocking his heart, preparing to say the one thing he'd vowed never to say to a woman again. 'I love you, Rio.'

Rio looked at Lysandros. He just stood there, the only sound the waves against the side of the speedboat. She tried to process the words she'd so wanted to hear, tried to replay them because she couldn't bear it if they weren't real, if he hadn't meant them.

He moved towards her suddenly, taking her arms, urging her to her feet to look at him, into his eyes. 'Did you hear me? I love you, Rio.'

Her heart soared high into the blue sky. He had said it.

He spoke rapidly in Greek, shocking her from her stunned silence. 'But I thought…' She stumbled over her words, unable to voice her confusion, her shock, but more importantly her love.

'I know what I told you. That I never wanted love in my life again.' He looked into her eyes, and love, mixed with fear of her rejection, shone from his. 'But you changed that, Rio. You, and I want this fake engagement to end too, because I want you to be my wife.'

His wife? Her head spun as fast as her heart thumped. 'You want to marry me? For real?'

'Yes.' He laughed, holding her hands as if afraid she might disappear, but she had no intention of going anywhere. The man she loved had told her he loved her. He'd left his past behind just as she had. 'I want to marry you. I want the woman I love with all my heart to be my wife—as soon as possible.'

He began to say something else but she pressed her finger to his lips, silencing him. Desire flooded his eyes and she smiled at him. 'I love you, Lysandros, but should we rush into this?'

'I've never been surer of anything in my life.'

'You really want to get married?'

'I do, Rio. I do.' Those words flashed through her mind. The look in his eyes heated her body and the love she'd suppressed since she'd come to the island overflowed.

'In that case, you'd better take me back to the island,' she teased.

'Not yet,' he said, pulling her into his arms. 'I think we should kiss and make up first.'

She smiled up at him as he bent to kiss her, a kiss that showed her just how much he loved her. She could feel it, taste it. His love wrapped itself around her, caressing her entire body. The kiss deepened and her body trembled with shock at his revelation and the unfurling heat of passion inside her.

'I love you so much,' she whispered against his lips, unsure if the swaying was her or the boat.

'Then marry me, not just be my fiancée. Say you will be my wife.'

She smiled at him as she pulled back, held safely in his arms, looking into his handsome face. 'Nothing would make me happier.'

He answered by drawing her close against him, kissing her until she melted with pleasure. His hands caressed her and she wished she could show him right now just how much she wanted him, how much she loved him.

'Why the hell aren't we on my yacht?' The feral growl of mock irritation made her laugh and the urge to taunt him was too strong to resist.

'And why would that be?' She couldn't keep the coy smile from her face, revelling in the power of his love.

'Because I want to make love to you—

right now. I want to prove to you how much I love you.'

'Then I will look forward to our wedding night.' Shyness made her blush and she looked down, away from the intensity in his eyes.

He lifted her chin back up gently, as he had done so many times. 'You are making me wait until we are married?'

'Yes,' she breathed in a husky whisper. 'And then I expect you to show me each and every night just how much you love me.'

His eyes darkened and the air became laden with desire. 'That will be my greatest pleasure.'

EPILOGUE

THE NEW SEASON for the orchestra was in full swing, and with Judith conducting, Rio had had no qualms about continuing her career. Xena too, fully recovered from the accident, was once more playing the violin.

Christmas was fast approaching and Rio had taken time off for a very important event. Xena and Ricardo were about to get married and Rome was filled with Christmas magic, the perfect setting for a wedding. It had also been the perfect setting in which to spend time with Lysandros.

As Xena and Ricardo had exchanged vows Rio had held Lysandros's hand. The small gathering of family members could be in no doubt that this couple belonged together as they were pronounced husband and wife. Rio looked up at Lysandros, standing beside her, remembering their intimate wedding day on the island at the end of the summer.

Only four months ago she had said the same words to him. It might not have been the big white church wedding she'd always dreamed of having, but the man she'd married far surpassed her dream. He was handsome and incredibly sexy, but far more than that, he cared for her and loved her.

Since that day on his speedboat when they had both put the past behind them, he had kept his promise, showing her just how much he loved her every day. Sometimes with passion that took her to another planet and sometimes with a gentle touch that held so much love.

He looked down at her as the happy couple turned to face their guests. 'Have I told you today just how beautiful you look?'

She smiled as he took her hand, pulling her against him, oblivious to those around him. 'Actually, you have,' she teased. 'At least a dozen times.'

'Come on, you two.' Xena's voice broke through the mist of desire that was building rapidly. 'We need you in the photographs.'

Lysandros smiled. 'I don't think we are going to be able to escape this. You know what Xena is like.'

'This is what she wanted all along,' said Rio

as she reluctantly moved away from her husband. 'Two happy-ever-afters.'

'You girls are such romantics.' Lysandros's voice was full of mock irritation as they joined the bride and groom for photographs outside the town hall in the winter sunshine.

As Rio stood beside her husband, making the perfect photo for Xena's wedding album, of brother and sister both finally happily married to their partners, she wondered how Lysandros would receive the news that he was to be a father.

He'd reassured her often that the past was exactly that and he wanted children, but as she'd done the pregnancy test yesterday, she'd worried it might be too soon. Despite that, excitement had filled her. She would tell him once they were alone.

'We have good news,' Xena said as they stood in their family group on the steps, posing for the photographs. 'Ricardo and I are expecting a baby.'

'I'm so happy for you,' Rio said excitedly. She and her best friend would become mothers together. They were now like sisters, and after all that Xena had been through to find her true love, Rio knew how much that would mean for the couple. 'When?'

'It's early days yet, but I just had to share

the news with you. Ricardo and I are expecting a summer baby.'

'There is only one thing that could please me more.' Lysandros added his congratulations as he shook Ricardo's hand, giving him a friendly slap on the back. 'And that would be to say the same thing to you.'

Rio took a deep breath before touching her husband's arm. When he looked down at her she nodded, the unspoken news bringing a smile to his face. She wanted to reassure him, to let him know the news they had both been tentatively hoping for was real. She didn't intend to take the spotlight from Xena's big day or announcement and hoped he would keep it quiet.

Lysandros, however, had other ideas. He picked her up, swinging her round, and when he set her back on her feet she looked at Xena, who wore that knowing smile. One so full of satisfaction and smugness that Rio couldn't help laughing.

'It appears that is exactly what I can say,' Lysandros said as Xena launched herself at him.

'I knew all along you two would make the perfect fairy tale,' Xena said, pulling away from Lysandros and taking Rio's hands.

The two of them looked at one another and Rio saw her friend's eyes were as full of love and happiness as she knew hers were. 'We both have that,' Rio said softly.

Xena hugged her as the two men congratulated one another. Then Lysandros took her in his arms and kissed her, leaving her in no doubt how pleased he was about the baby.

As Xena tried to restore order to the unruly group photograph, Lysandros smiled at his wife, that desire-laden darkness in his eyes. 'I love you, Rio Drakakis, and I couldn't be happier. I'm going to be a father.'

Rio's heart soared. From a disastrous moment in London and a terrible accident had come total happiness for her and Xena. A perfect ending.

* * * * *

If you enjoyed
Seducing His Convenient Innocent,
you're sure to enjoy these other stories
by Rachael Thomas!

Valdez's Bartered Bride
Martinez's Pregnant Wife
Hired to Wear the Sheikh's Ring
A Ring to Claim His Legacy

Available now!